TWO NOVELLAS

Twilight And The Migrant

PROF. DHARAMPAL PASRICHA

PARTRIDGE
A Penguin Company

Partridge books may be ordered through booksellers or by contacting:

Partridge India
Penguin Books India Pvt.Ltd
11, Community Centre, Panchsheel Park, New Delhi 110017
India
www.partridgepublishing.com
Phone: 000.800.10062.62

TWO NOVELLAS

Special Thanks to **Ashu Nagpal, Mohini** and **Shalini**.

The novel 'Twilight' captures glimmering and hazy landscapes of politics in India. It has bright and dark spots. It enables the reader to have a peep into the intricate situations in Indian poilitics. Agitations in India do not succeed unless supported by political big-wigs. Political leaders shake all principles and politicize human situations. Victims of political riots are left to their disasterous fate.

The novel has universal appeal and has something for every reader.

Invocation

(Shri Radha-Krishna)
Inspired by
(Nitin, Poonaashu, Siddarth and Divya)

TWILIGHT

(Glimmering And Hazy Landscapes Of Indian Politics)

Prof. Dharam Pal

1

He sat near the treble of a tap fixed up somewhere on the verge of a patched-up street. A lone figure! The mid-day was filtering itself through a zig-zag of clouds in the sky. Brooding mid-day! Suddenly the tap sucked up the last drops of water creating a small, arid landscape through it. The doors were bolted, chained from within lending an aspect of fear to the most frequented street of the town. By-lanes stood tranquil as if deprived of last signs of any kind of life. Rajeev fluttered his eye-lids in the manner of a fugitive. He could have stayed inside the doors making himself less vulnerable to the rioters. They had spared him the throb of his life. They could have crushed him into pulp. He felt racked and emotionally frayed. It was a monumental effort for him to collect himself. His lone, sane voice of protest against violence in the town was thrown away to silent, ominous winds present in the lanes like a hunted beast.

One of the rioters had slapped Rajeev across his jaws. 'You crazy mad-man get out of our way or . . .'

'Spare him. He does not know what he talks.'

Perching near the tap he could visualize the group of violent faces registering their yells, expressing their 'devil may care attitude.'

They seemed to be a determined lot as if sponsored by Devil himself. Destruction was writ large in their eyes and they carried ignition material with them.

He had stood facing Ajeet, confronting his scattered visage with beastly actions. Ajeet had paused and given the look of a maddened beast out for prowling in the wilderness of civilization. He had poured his venom at him, 'Hell, with you . . . Rajeev. You hardly understand revolution . . .'

'Revolution!' For Rajeev the word was too absurd in the present circumstances.

'Rajeev, I say don't oppose me. I say, you get away or I'll thrash you. Don't blame. You bloody shit . . .'

'Don't destroy the town . . .'

'The town does not belong to you . . . does it? Tell me . . . does it?'

The contours of his head conglomerated in a number of agitated lines. Rajeev, for a moment, was seized of a mortal fear. Yet he went on with his pleadings lost in the yell of the mob. Ajeet had pushed him aside violently verging on a poignant hatred for this young man. Loathing for him was sinister and could be traced back to many situations full of tension and mutual mistrust. The rioter had forced shopkeepers to draw their shutters in a huff and bewilderment.

Rajeev saw a man running breathlessly as if in swoon. He shouted at his racing back, 'why don't you stop? Stop, give me the story you seem to be desperate, why? I say why don't you stop?'

He did stop in the way for a linger.

'Why, what's wrong?' Rajeev approached him with hasty steps.

'They are burning . . .' he gasped.

'Burning? what burning?

You don't understand. You stand in a by-lane. Go in the open. Overthere . . . 'His eyes moved from one direction to the other like the swing of a pendulum.

'Why . . . they have put the railway station, the post-office on fire . . . big fire . . . all spreading fire . . . ?'

'Any one there to prevent them?'

'Oh . . . No . . . no authority . . . no police . . . no official . . . only smoke rising . . .'

'I'll go there.'

'You . . . oh! yes, yes . . . go there. Fire would not care for you or stop for you. Don't go there. No one is around. Only a handful of them. Spoiled, wild animals.'

He raced away like a maniac leaving Rajeev to his broodings. The doors of houses and shops were slammed. Not a soul stirring.

Rajeev sat down on one of the steps of a nearby house. A neglected dog came and sat near him like an audience to a tale. Clouds did not disperse. They gained strength by huddling to-gether and lengthened their shadows over roof-tops.

Ajeet's face emerged in Rajeev's sub-conscious like a black spot. It was quite easy for him to reconstruct Ajeet's past. Their to-getherness had been like eclipsed nettled sun-beams. Why shouldn't he go to spots of devastations?

Let him be a witness to the actual of burning. At least he will be able to make his presence felt there. Like an escapist he should not sit and want for the turn of the situation. Was he an escapist? He made an attempt to search his real-self. They could have killed him in the excited, furious stampede. Providential escape ! He felt the sinews of his shoulders and found them in ache. He had received a hurt from one of the iron-bars in the mob.

He started plodding through lanes. Some house-doors stood ajar and he could locate eyes stuck to crevices of the doors. They wouldn't come out. Self-preservation is the basic instinct bequeathed to us by nature. He imaginatively heard their whispers subdued by panic and something sinister.

A lapse of some moments and he found himself on the road leading to the railway station. He saw distant patches of smokes diluted by the vastness of the sky. Emotional wilderness ! the words popped up in his sub-conscious like the fall of a stone in the still pond. He looked back and found the partly depreciated dog following him. He bent down to peer into the eyes of the animal. It too halted putting a lot of pressure on its hunches and was not scared of him. The road was almost deserted without any rising of dust. They must have scared humans and animals to their hidings.

Lo . . . there was a yell—a bovine unison of the rioters. They must be busy putting buildings on fire and deriving a lot of morbid pleasure. Unconsciously he muttered to the dog 'Devil has found a place in their hearts. Once frenzy is on . . . man runs amuck. Consequences? Hell with the consequences.'

The dog blinked it's eye-lids and it's ears were taut with tension. There was a crash and din of a great magnitude. He looked around to locate the sight of the noise, but it was not within sight.

A few moments of walking took him to the spot of crash.

Ajeet was there surrounded by a furious mob of not a very large number. Their faces aglow with their immediate victories in devastation. They imparted the impression of having done something heroic and noble. One of them shouted, 'Look over there the post office. I put it on fire. My dream has come true.' The short-sized boy was bubbling in enthusiasm. 'So you have come here also. You Rajeev, I'm talking to you. Yes . . . only to you. Don't look here and there. Can you pacify us? You just can't.' And Ajeet walked in the direction of Rajeev with an air of defiance putting him on the defensive.

'You can't attack me . . . you see . . . Ajeet.'

Rajeev uttered the sentence with a lot of poise.

'Why? . . . we can attack any one who crosses our way . . . yes . . . anyone . . .' Ajeet's face was flushed with unusual anger and indignation.

'You can't prevent us . . . By the way. Are you a stoog . . . of some *Neta*? There is no one around us. You understand?'

'That does not mean you destroy the property of the nation.'

'Nation? A sardonic smile fell upon Ajeet's face lit with a perverted sense of victory over his adversary.

'Rajeev, don't cross my way. O.K. You mind your own business. Don't play with fire. I spare you only because you happen to be a classmate. Go your own way. Read books and live in the bookish morality.'

Ajeet stammered in anger and hatred. The movement of his lips did not coincide with powerful ejaculation of venom, hatred and cunning harboured by this man. Rajeev was fixed up in a moment of insecurity. He peered at Ajeet's face as if in a state of delirium. The face stood with its rough contours tracing their furrows from his temples to his chin. His eye-lids kept on blinking in a mysterious manner within giving an inkling as to what was passing in his mind.

'You chase us like a dog. We avoid killing men. We know each other . . . that's why?'

Ajeet and his accomplices were in a mood to quit. It was followed by a ruffle of human heads at a distance. They did not want to be seen. They scattered away like pack of cards. Rajeev stayed back for the ruffle to be identified.

It neared and identified a group of paratroopers hastening to the troubled spots in the town. Rajeev felt enraged at their relaxed faces. The entire town has been kept on the edge of sword for two hours. 'And by the way what are you doing here? Don't you see the town in fire?

'I say, you get away . . . get away . . . otherwise . . .' a hoarse, sulky voice struck Rajeev's ears.

'I have been waiting for you.'

'What the hell do you talk? Rubbish waiting for you? By the way . . . who are you? *Laat Sahab* . . .' the voice betrayed a greater share of anger.

'They have run away . . . Sir!'

'Can't understand you? Do you find anyone here? Get . . . inside . . . or law will . . . '

Rajeev gave a jerky push to his voice, 'You always come late. Always. It's already burnt and smashed. Where were you when Ajeet and his boys were creating fire in the town?'

The horseman's agitation was mounting beyond endurance. A kind of rhythm was set-up between the horse and the rider.

'Don't back. Get going. We have orders. Who the hell are you? I say, who the hell . . .'

'Me? just a common fellow. I fear against violence. Don't I have a right to feel . . . ?'

'By the way . . . why should you feel? You just get lost. Otherwise law will take its own course.'

Rajeev peered into horseman's eyes. 'That's the irony. Law proceeds against the innocent. That's the problem.'

'Whoever you may be. We have no time for you. Get away. Otherwise I'll beat you at the policestation.

The horseman's voice carried a lot of threat for Rajeev.

'You look like a student. Don't spoil your record. I don't wish to spoil your future. You see that's why.'

The horseman gave him a very stern look. A look that betrayed something sinister in it. Rajeev was a but apprehensive of what could happen.

We do not wish to be punished for nothing. So he moved in the direction opposite to the beat of the uniformed group. The horseman jerked the reins of the horse to join his clan.

Rajeev's sub-conscious built-up an image of the departed horseman. His nostrils were kept wide awake during the altercation. He had positioned himself in an aggressive posture on the verge of thrashing him.

'Yes . . . I had a narrow escape. A day of narrow escapes.' He muttered to himself. He troded along the semi-paved road leading in the interior of the town. Impulsively he looked around to locate the creature quiet and barking. Yes, it was there like enlarged speck under the opaque sun. Suddenly he felt that the town was blistered all over its body and some of the blisters were on the verge of foul-smelling eruptions. He beckoned the innocent creature to give place to its slow, brooding stepping forward. As its presence gave some sense of belongingness. A kind of relationship that develops suddenly without any preface to the book. At least he wasn't that lonely. Loneliness is a sort of storm that flows in all directions. It brings to us various landscapes of our own psyche.

He must go home. The warning of the horseman echoed loudly in his sub-conscious.

The early evening was taking shapes according to the structures on the land. He wondered how cosmic forces take shapes in the world of human beings. Cosmic forces have their independent, vital existence and act according to their own inherent laws. Yet their connections can not be totally snapped with human beings.

Shops were closed, but some stray men came within his sight. He felt like talking to them. Why didn't they come out and protest? He wondered at the indifference of common people. They were just indifferent. Others will manage for them. They needn't risk anything. Time, money, security are the main consideration with the masses. Their own problems are quite important and absorbing.

How could Gandhi muster support of masses? Must be something divine in him. No . . . no . . . he rejected his own way of thinking. Nothing divine. Gandhi's ways of thinking and action were outcome of self-discipline without any axe to grind. He infused a spirit of sacrifice in masses because of his own dedication to a cause.

It was something from within, from his self that revolted against injustice. Gandhi was interested neither in science nor in literature but in human beings. Love for man brought him to a gruesome death. He walked upto an odd trio discussing in an odd corner. They just blinked their eyes at his approach.

'Only a handful of them burnt important points in the town. Thank God, they didn't come to our side. We feared their attack on our locality . . . also . . .'

The speaker was of middle-age and his beaten face betrayed a lot of fear on it.

'We didn't come out. You see . . . just peeped out . . . once or twice. Peeped out and slammed the doors.

'Did you hear any noise?'

'I learn it was not a big group. Just a handful. Why didn't police come out? Why don't they catch hold anti-social idiots?'

Rajeev was silent listening him.

A back-door conspiracy. Political. Some man behind the closed-doors. They say it's some leader out to have political advantage. The man grew quite frozen as if he were exposed to some danger from his immediate surroundings.

'Why didn't you come out to protest? Strange. Shocking. Just a handful of them.'

Rajeev spoke the words like a defeatist. His face registered a lot of consternation, helplessness born out of a hopeless situation. He continued struggling within himself with some black patches in his sub-conscious.

Intricine struggle of a thinking man! Thoughts embroiled in the cob-webs of contradictions!

'And why shouldn't we come out? why? After all we don't have to lose our lives. Life is precious to us. Very precious . . .' His fluttering eye-lids were in activity and were purposely avoiding the speaker. The trio made gestures to get rid of the new arrival. But Rajeev stuck to his guns. He looked at each one of them as if to anticipate their reactions. He focused his intent glance on one of them.

'We have forgotten how to protest peacefully. Passive spectactors, pressed with our own problems.

We are either passive or turn into violent mobs . . .'

The three gave him evasive hearing. They didn't want any discussion except criticism of the authorities for not dealing with the situation promptly. Only 'they' are responsible.

One of them interposed stammeringly, 'By the way . . . gentleman . . . who are we to interfere? Just tell me . . . why should we get killed? Why? who will look after our children?'

He moved his eyes on their faces like a spider and tried to seek their faces. One of the trio came to the rescue of the speaker 'Our protest doesn't matter. You see . . . people are not united. Everyone for himself. Simple rule.' The dog stood there as if trying to follow the discussion. It looked at Rajeev as if asking him to depart from this place.

Rajeev and the dog followed a broad road. Their hasty steps took them in the direction of straight, wide, road leading to Rajeev's home.

Suddenly his attention was caught up by an unusual glow at some distance. The road lay expectant and quieter with a lot of litter lying on both the sides. The glow was proceeding in the opposite direction of his walking. He was hushed up inwardly. O God ! it was a speeding vehicle emitting flames in all directions. There was a crash, a din giving a jolt to the atmosphere. Rajeev was at the spot after a few more bouncing steps. The bus lay scattered against a way-side tree like an injured visitor. The impact of the collusion was severe scalding of the various parts of such situations. They must be around. After all they have a responsibility . . .'

He raised his head to see the person standing nearby him. He got up putting a lot of strain to his knees.

'Ghastly accident of the day.' A voice squeaked out of the group.

'Never witnessed such incidents. My stay in this town is of more than forty years. But such a situation . . . oh . . . no . . . never.' The old man did not fumble for such words though his teeth looked like a barren land.

The boy is a dare devil. Who did prompt him? Of course . . . a dare devil ! surprising . . . shocking. The town reduced to a burning *ghat.*'

'It's all the doing of a politician. Must be for some political gain.'

Rajeev was led to a sort of mental psychosis. How to inform the parents of the dead boy? Should he himself go or let the police take its course? But it may take long before the body reaches its destination.

People were converging reluctantly at the sight in twos and threes, as if they were about to enter a danger zone. The sight of devastation began to swell with mute and chattering faces.

'Oye . . . Oye . . . I know him . . . yes . . . yes . . . He lives in Krishna Colony. Krishna Colony . . .'

'Parents . . . old . . . and poor. Second death in the family. Only brother of three sisters . . .' Another voice echoed in the crowd.

'*Hai-Bhagwan* this boy! I know him since childhood, only help to his family.'

'Let's take the dead body . . .'

'Where?'

'To Krishna colony . . . to his old, poor parents.'

'How about the police case?'

'No one around. Jungle law. The dead body will rot here. No police . . . no . . . *kanoon . . .*'

There was a pall of dismay shrouding the emotional contours of the crowd.

The dog was already there . . . perched near the dead body in a posture of perfect silence.

Rajeev looked at the mute creature that had followed him since their encounter in the by-lanes.

There was an implied consent in the crowd that Krishna's dead body should be removed to his house. Apprehensions regarding the legal procedure stayed back in their minds. Rajeev stepped forward and slid his arm under the charred neck.

A commotion in the crowd and some stepped forward to lend a hand to the lifting of the body.

It look the shape of a scattered procession. Dumb faces. Slow and unsteady movement. Something sinister sat on their faces. Conglomeration of sub-conscious fears, a sense of insecurity and fear of the unseen created an awe of its own kind. Rajeev almost visualized a picture of gloom shattering everyday contours of Krishna's house.

One of them stepped forward and almost yelled, 'Yes . . . over there . . . The lane ends on a square. From the right. Yes, right. A new lane starts. It terminates in Krishna's house.'

Their arrival at the lane resulted in the movement of hurrying steps coming out of their houses like bees swarming an enclosure. Their anxiety to be one with the situation was overflowing. A shop-keeper shouted 'who is burnt? who . . . Krishna? My God ! he lives here. He is burnt like coal.'

The muddy lane had developed cracks like sudden eruptions on a human body. Krishna Colony with its zig-zag patches, half-broken lay mired and tranquil. Krishna's house did not have spacious doors. Their dimensions betrayed the contents and the inmates of the house.

'We can stay here. We can't crowd the house. Stop-stop, not more than twenty people.'

The surging crowd stood restless.

Rajeev went ahead of the group treasuring the dead body. A slow, sudden knock at the door with prominent crevices permitting tiny whiffs of wind. Rajeev felt like a patient under anesthesia.

The knock was repeated with a sub-dued pitch. Two worn out, dim eyes peeped through one of the slits on the door. He took time to unlatch the door and stood peering at Rajeev. Many moments of painful silence followed the door. His scanty eye-lids fluttered revealing the little orbes of his light half extinguished.

'Who are you? who . . . they?' The old man's words crawled punctuated by a big stifle.

'Krishna . . .' Rajeev muttered the name creeping up an outer poise.

The old man whispered, 'Krishna? Not at home. We are waiting . . . waiting . . .'

He could not hide his anxiety. Rajeev began to sob and a few others joined the sub-dued wail. Before the old man could make out the grim situation, they entered the low ceiling dinghy scant of full light and breath of air. The inmates did recognise the cleared face and their desperation took a lonely, sudden wailing beyond endurance. The old, shattered mother was almost propped up by the three sisters. They fell upon his body crying and making frantic gesticulations as if to rescue him from his present state. There was no point of return.

Rajeev sat tranquil near the moment of eternity. He made abortive attempts to console the family but it proved beyond him. The old man was a crumpled, heap of sorrow.

A drizzle at the moment was like the most unwelcomed guest at mid-night. The outsiders sought shelter under tiny sheds and way-side projections. They were waiting for Krishna's last rites. But why didn't they come out to face the rioters? Rajeev pondered in snatches over the issue. They have forgotten the language of peaceful protest. They have forgotten Gandhi's language. But what about Krishna. He must have been in frenzy. A frenzy fuelled in him by his surroundings.

'Let's prepare for his cremation. People can't wait. Weather is getting out of hand?'

Some one of them suggested rather meekly. It sent a vibration of warning and the waiting came to a sudden halt. He must be taken away from the house where he had spent twenty years of his life. Dispatched from the earth for no fault of his own.

Strife, torn town, devastated by a handful of rioters ! Who will take care of Krishna's family? The question assumed a glooming shape in Rajeev's sub-conscious. Krishna's father was non-entity and his mother a wasted human frame. The three sisters all beautiful and attractive. They were picking up for the final scene of Krishna's life.

'Hurry-up . . . hurry-up . . .' a blinking middle aged man tried to make his presence felt.

The dog was there sequestered in a corner at the thresh-hold waiting for the funeral procession to start. Rajeev looked at it and wondered at its fidelity. After all why should he follow him?

Animals have an uncanny sense for human beings and situations. We, humans, hardly find any time to understand them and go into animal psyche.

The procession took the direction and road to the nearest burial ground. There was hardly any mirth and hospitality in the surroundings. The sky was drenched, overloaded and hung like a leaking canopy. Krishna's father was supported by two men as it was almost impossible for the dreary figure to take a step forward. His legs hung like two sticks balancing a tattering table.

Rajeev's mind went into philosophical ramblings and he came upon his favourite contemplation, man set against the vastness of the universe. Yet the tiny human brain carries consciousness of the vast, endless universe. Twenty years grown body was given to flames rising toward the sky. The sky didn't receive any tarnish because of the smoke from the burnt out ends of the day.

2

A car was moving along the muddy, broken, cracked path. The landscape lay scattered around consisting of sprawling fields, still, grim trees. There was hardly any movement in the leaves. The whole of the moon was there under a big bundle of packed up clouds rendering the night partially opaque. In the mighty movement a ray or two streaked out along the distant rims of the sky. The firmament of the sky seemed to be oozing in the partial darkness.

The occupant of the car was silent, lost and fixed with the day's happenings in the city. How could he help the riff-raff? The burnt precincts of the city were distantly visible to him. It is a part of the game. He chuckled to himself and adjusted his cap on his bald-pate. The movement of the car was rather slow. He could not help it. He reassured himself on the verge of a nagging.

He mumbled to himself, 'Politics being what it is today. We belong to the same flock. All of them raise strikes, *dharnas*, rigging, bribing, ballot-box lifting and what not? Why should he feel guilty?'

The car came to a sudden halt.

'*Shahab*, very bad path. Pits and pits.' The driver's complaint was low-pitched.

'Ram Singh, try your best. I must reach there. It's quite important. They are waiting for me.'

'Yes . . . *Shahab* . . . ?'

The car made a whirring sound and lurched out like a snail. There was the cry of an owl.

'Bad omen' . . . the occupant rather spoke to himself.

'What does it forecast?' his palm moved on his rough forehead touching drops of sweat.

'Did you speak to me . . . *Shahab*?'

'No' the leader was a bit taken aback at his own mumblings. There they were. A small room at the receding ends of the town. A distance of five kilometers. A small room invisible to the casual, inattentive, naked eye. Cow-dung plastered room.

Sooryakant came out of his car, adjusted his cap and headed towards the room. It was a very narrow-mud path, he trod upon. A bit difficult for him to balance his bulging paunch.

Ajeet was the first to walk towards the political figure. His face presented an aspect of dismay and expectation. His furrowed forehead was glaring because of the lines on it. '*Namskaar* . . .' his folded hands welcomed Sooryakant.

'I did my best. Almost all public buildings burnt or left half unburnt. Fear, tension, rumour in the town. What else do you want? Our project is a complete success!'

The leader was already seated on an old chair and was attentive to the flow of news.

'Police did not interfere. They arrived after our job was over. They didn't identify us.' Ajeet drew an immense satisfaction at his brilliant performance. The incumbent of the chair was more interested in listening to Ajeet than expressing anything of his own. He seemed to be assured of his supremacy as a background to the chain of events since morning. The town was already in the grip of intense tension prone silence. The only way to defeat his political rivals. He reflected inwardly. His awareness did not go beyond this. There was an air of causality to his active broodings.

'Krishna's body reduced to ashes. None of our faults. No one prompted him.

'It was n't our scheming.' Ajeet's voice echoed sharply.'

There followed many moments of silence. The moon was already out of the grip of packed-up clouds . . . crops were beginning to feel the presence of light wind. A slow creeping commotion suddenly spread upon the entire aspect of the tranquil night. Overthere, at a distance, stood a group of trees seemed to be declining in sizes.

'Any suspicions around the town?' the simple, clad man picked up the conversation.

'The town is hot with rumours. All sorts of rumours. They sense a political hand behind the upheaval.'

'What about Rajeev? The one who does not co-operate with you.'

'O . . . Rajeev? He does not matter much. We snubbed him. Lonely and forsaken ! An argument here and there does not matter.'

'Correct. Arguments don't matter these days. We must go beyond all this idealogical non-sense.'

'We are successful, Sir,' Ajeet beat with triumph. A brief smile flitted across his broad face. His eye-lids made a quick flutter.

'You'll be amply rewarded.' the leader got up from the seat. How about your friends?'

'Wellfed, protected. They are busy drinking.'

'Take care of these fellows. They will also be rewarded. Useful. You stand a fair chance . . . if I come in power. Keep watch on Rajeev.'

'We are quite vigilant. He is a thinking sort. He talks of healthy democracy, equal rights and what not. Crazy fellow !'

Ajeet followed Sooryakant through mazy fields. The moon stood naked in the sky. There seemed to be a sense of mystery of which they seemed to be unaware.

'People must understand my opponent's failure. He is unable to contain violence.

'We have managed it at the most appropriate time. Yes . . . the most appropriate time. We must strike, otherwise nothing clicks.'

Sooryakant did not expect Ajeet to reply but to listen. His pace was slow but well managed. He did not give the impression of being impatient. He stopped and looked back. Ajeet's face was not explicit to him.

'You see . . . it takes time to mature things. I had already instructed the D.S.P. to play traunt with the situation. I got him promoted.

'You see . . . we need one another. Only foolish young men like Rajeev expect a fair play.'

Ajeet nodded. They were almost nearing the car. Ram Singh looked a bit scarred of the former minister.

'Ajeet, here is money for you. Leave the room by dawn. Don't stay back. They may harm you. You see people in power also understand. There is C.I.D. though I have my men in the set-up. We should be cautions.'

The car started with the emission of a lot of smoke. Ajeet put the bundle of currency notes some where under his vest. Leadership never goes wasted. Once you indulge in politics, things begin to move in a big way, what is the use of mere bookish knowledge? Big leaders can't manage everything by themselves. Ajeet paused on the narrow-path. His experience of college elections, wasted? No. His quarrels with his teachers? No. Experience Counts. Big leaders have to depend upon young leaders.

Ajeet was back to his clan. Their faces were flushed with wine. Tremulous tongues wagged like a pebbled stream in a huge, dense forest.

'Ajeet . . . you are a wonderful man. A great leader and our benefactor.' The speaker was drowned in the unity of his performance of burning in the city. His teeth clattered like small chunks of rough stones. He looked at Ajeet with an air of gratitude. 'Minister gives you money. Wonderful.'

'That's what we want. It serves well. Money, wine . . . and . . . and . . .'

'And . . . ?' one of them questioned with a cunning laugh.

'And . . . women . . .'

'By God . . .'

'Don't worry. That will come. Only Rajeev can prattle foolishly about idealogy. What did he say? The other day he said movement of any kind should be pious. Holy. Then it works. Always quoting Gandhi.

'Foolish . . . Irrelevant . . .'

'He says Gandhi never started a movement for his own ends.'

'Forget Rajeev and his Gandhi. Let them rest in books.'

'Books? foolish and unpractical.' There arose a mild laughter in the company.

'Ajeet, you're superb. You involve us in any kind of protest, movement.'

'Violent or non-violent, what matters are the benefits, wine, women and . . .'

'It's simply marvelous. Put up a tent. Two boys in the centre with garlands around them. So called fasting. A few banners. Collection of funds. Lecturing and then drinking at night . . .'

'Professional agitators . . . It's a nice profession.'

Intoxicated minds waited for the question to be answered. Their tongues clicked like the forked tongue of a snake.

'And then drink at night. Enjoy the best food. Bribe the policeman on duty. Some glasses of fine liquor serves them right. After all they are also humans. They need some diversion.'

'Movements are a lucrative profession. You enjoy the part of both the worlds. Money, wine and women and reputation.' High-pitched laughter floated for sometime. No pang of conscience, ideology or any other moral snag troubled them. They were in a bovine state of mind with continuous aerobatic gestures.

'Will those golden days come back Ajeet?'

'Don't worry. India is full of problems. She gives ample opportunities to tents.'

'Rajeev says . . .'

'Hell with Rajeev . . .' the speaker was snapped and crushed.

'No check on freedom of speech . . .'

'O . . . yes . . . what does Rajeev say?'

'He says these days people are protesting even when the causes are casual, selfish, harmful, and Rajeev says . . . Rajeev says . . . why don't you stop him from saying. At least I'm fed-up. Rajeev says . . . You are obsessed. How many pegs?'

'Why . . . everything in your presence.' I'm not gone beyond five. What about you?'

'Didn't keep a count . . .'

'Rajeev says Gandhi always found out moral implications before launching movements. During the movement he observed a strict personal and social sanctity. He allowed nothing commoral to creep in.'

Unusual silence. Was it recollection of Gandhi or an overintoxicated state of mind?

At least they were unaware of the ruffle among leaves outside the room. Since the departure of the car, the sky had assumed many new facets. A pale, hazy moon was proceeding towards a gradual decline. May be it was the initiation of dawn bringing distant trees into dim focus. A gradual rising light seemed to be divesting them of their darkness.

Silence inside the room did not continue for long. Ajeet instructed them regarding the future course of action. He peeped into their half-dazed, intoxicated eyes and he spoke in well-arranged words.

'Sooryakant is pleased with your co-operation. He has already paid you handsome dividends. He assures us of more money.'

'Well done . . . Ajeet. What are we fighting for? Money. For us there is no other way to settle . . . As students we passed our examinations through copying. I am certain we can become very successful leaders. What do you think?'

Thousands clapping and yelling's pierced the early dawn.

'Everyone has his own way of doing things. Moreover, we don't achieve anything. We have our own talents. I'll manage certificates for you. Why should we waste our precious time reading books? We are on a greater mission in our life. Don't you follow?'

'Certificates? How will you manage degrees for us?'

'Don't worry. That's for me to plan. We can plan burning of a town. Managing certificates is not difficult.'

They clapped to approve satanic utterances of their leader. A riotous pandemonium expressing their intoxicated nerves was created in the small room. Money was distributed by Ajeet. It was almost performing a ritual.

'I'm a link between you and the leader . . .'

There followed a wild clapping in the smoke-suffocated room. They bundled their bets and left the room before the sunlight could penetrate the thin pall of pre-dawn darkness.

3

Rajeev entered Krishna's house with a lot of sorrow poised on his face. He felt guilty, depressed and trodden-upon. Most of the rituals of Krishna's cremation were already performed. His parents were in a state of shock beyond recognition. The old man was in a state of bewilderment often bewailing. "Rajeev, you are like son to me. Tell me how did Krishna die? I am confounded, helpless. Who is responsible? who will take to us? Who?"

The mother also joined. Ajeet is to blame. She came there and talked to Rajeev in a corner, "Do you also belong to them?"

Rajeev's tone had a sob in it. 'They do not like me. They do not like my thinking. Mother, I was expelled. I tried to win over Krishna but he did not bother. Where was the bravery in driving a burning bus?' He ate the words as his tears rolled in pent-up gush. 'You see Krishna would not listen, I wish he would listen but, but . . .' There was perceptible sobbing in the room.

Krishna's youngest sister Smita found some room for herself behind the door. Only her eyes staring in the vacancy were visible. In them there was a constant flow of tears. Her eye-lashes were dipped like wings of butterfly. Her stare became constant at Rajeev's dismayed face. A single flutter in her eyelids. Communication was set up between the two following a deep stirring in their sub-conscious. Smita's face had prominent contours of being romantic and prosaic. A curious combination of dream and reality! Her voice was melodious and at times resounding. The moment, two were electrically charged and for a while lifted them out of their routine, settled existence. At the moment Rajeev was in the grip of something grim and sorrowful. He had been a witness to the spectacle of devastation and anguished thoughts. Ajeet was to blame. He became a convenient tool in the hands of a defeated politician and created a clan for him. He was about to get up from Charpoy when Smita caught him with a meaningful grace. May be she needed words of consolation from him! Why not to go and talk to her? For the fiirst time, he felt shy talking to her. Why? He was bewildered at his own sensitive self-consciousness. Was it because of his new-born feelings for her? He questioned himself like an analyst. The old man's words in his ears. How to carry on the burden of the family? Old age is a curse. What can I do now? Krishna the only bread-earner is gone for ever.

His sobbings became louder than his emaciated body could afford.

'The Government will repair public buildngs. Who will repair my loss?'

The old man was almost on the verge of swooning.

'We'll do something for you father.'

What will you do?'

'I can not tell you. It will take some time.'

He intently looked at the man and left the Charpoy to join Smita inside the room. She stood behind the half-shut door. Her bright face was scarred by her profouse weepings. He discerned a kind of volatile sensitivity on her face. For the first time he found some streaks of uncanny beauty on her face. Perhaps normal looks do not capture the hidden and the essential. We form routine usual pictures of human-beings in our routine contact.

'How could you neglect us for that long?' Smita's question was abrupt.

Her thinking coloured her face. Suddenly he found the old man attentive to him 'Beta Rajeev, does it behove daughters to earn for the old father?'

He looked at the two daughters, fluttered his eyelids and focussed on Rajeev. He was in affix. Should he support the old man or his daughters? The old man should be encouraged to wash off his sense of guilt. Otherwise tension will live in the house.

'You are Gandhi's agitators?' She smiled. There was a free flow of emotion between the two. Their eyes held each other in a focus of happiness. The room was partially dark because of the slant in the entry of the sun-rays. The roof of the room was low and did not allow a direct view of the enterant to the room. In this room she had her moments of loneliness, cutting off from the general flow of humanity. At times you seem to be different from others. A queer sort! The common folk are connected with physical, tangible without an awareness. They just complete routine. Rajeev spoke to Smita.

'You talk philosophy . . .'

'That is fine . . .' Smita raised a small giggle.

He enclosed her face with his palms and then sought her glance.

She kept her eyes-lashes in down-cast posture. Her eyes-lids did not show any movement.

These days lovers are so practical. There is no feeling between the two. She gave a slight nod to her head without lifting her face. And then Smita suddenly lifted her face looking at Rajeev deep and long. She seemed to be overwhelmed and bit panting. She managed to mutter, 'you say things after my heart, Rajeev.'

'Really?'

'You never betray them explicitly.'

'A girl is supposed to keep mum.'

'Why?'

'Should I explain woman psychology to you?'

'No harm.'

The two words echoed in his ears. Rekha and Sona the other two sisters sauntered in quietly. A flush on their faces. Smita and Rajeev gave the impression of being caught red-handed. Sona's tone carried a bit of scarcasm. Smita must be talking books to him. They talk films. Rekha too joined conversation, crazy after films. A smart young hero singing to a beautiful girl or they singing together. Films carry beautiful girls, sights, falls, mountains and the open sky. At least on the screen. Rajeev spoke with unusual grimness. 'I am not interested in movies, same stuff, mere artificial. Why not to start an agitation?'

Smita and her sisters were taken aback. The atmosphere hung with tension and suspicion. Rajeev threw them into enormous curisoity. 'why? It is to demand justice for Krishna's death.'

Suddenly a pall of dismay descended upon the company. They were left pondering to a bootless inquisitiveness.

'Sorry to remind you of Krishna. An agitation for the right cause. There was a conspiracy behind his death. Someone behind the scene. Krishna's death should not go unaccounted for.'

'We are not stuff for agitations. Who will listen to us?' Smita expressed her doubts.

'Agitations for the right cause, For justice. How did Gandhi manage his agitations? Did he possess some extra powers? He was a commoner.' Rajeev's tone was firm. It was different with him. 'He did not fight for himself. He fought for others. Masses supported him. Issues and aims were clear.'

'No, I do not agree with you.'

'Rajeev, Times have changed. Now agitations are taken in stride.' Smita was persistent with her argument.

Rajeev was quiet and was left to a state of inner uncertainty. A fight within and a fight without. There should be a tuning between the two. Otherwise the balance between the two is lost.

Sona interposed suddenly. 'We are more concerned with work and bread. Some work, some kind of engagement to keep on going.'

Her voice was punctuated with sentimental ups and downs. What could they do? Poverty sat staring at their door blankly at them and Rajeev thought of an agitation. Krishna could not be brought back with an agitation. He was gone to the land of no return.

'It s not only Krishna's death. It is to draw attention to innocent deaths. The country is full of them. Human life thrown to dogs. Just like that.'

'Who is responsible?' Smita's glance was deep and bewitching. The other two looked with their eyes down-cast.

'Why should we follow our leaders blindly? A wave in the religion or any other blind cause sweeps them along.'

'But without protest issues do not surface. These do not catch the public eyes.

'That's necessary. I understand causes for agitations should be selfless. These days agitations are for self glorificaton and to establish leadership and not for the welfare of masses.'

Sona and Rekha were not interested in this intellectual see-saw. They hardly bothered about things beyond their immediate existence. How to sustain their existence? The moot question ate them like a canker. Smita's mind pondred over issues and was given to daydreaming.

'How do you take the idea of going on fast?'

'I don't exactly know. Will it succeed?'

Clouds of doubt hung in the room. Sona and Rekha walked out of the room without uttering a word. There was no idea in talking to the couple.

'Have you worked out the implications of fasting Rajeev?'

'We have to make a beginning. Any more friends?'

'I shall talk. Political parties are ready. But . . .'

'But'

'Let us not politicize Krishna's death.'

As such Smita did not take any interest in politics.

She was a thinking sort and always maintained an inner identity.

'At times you say things unexpected of your age, Smita.' Rajeev often told her.

For a while there was a meaningful silence in the room. They seemed to be stuggling with their ideas.

'I feel fasting as a protest becoming out-dated and meaningless. Most of us believe protests are a humbug. Just a contrivance.'

'May be loss of faith in Gandhi's methods.'

'Why, there are other methods to raise protest strikes? *Dharnas*? Violence?"

'No, the only sensible way is to remain non-violent, the only way of fighting.'

Rajeev was moved beyond words. He was charged with emotion. Leaders like Ajeet must be fought as they were multiplying in numbers. Their aims were wicked. Rajeev knew that his struggle was going to be lonesome one. Most of them were with Ajeet. He had means and funds to satisfy their low desires. But why did Krishna back Ajeet? Ajeet mght have taken him into his gang because of his lust for his sisters.

4

The evening was waning into night when Rajeev went to see Smita. She was in the room concentrating over a book. Her face looked seriously composed. Two of her sisters sat with their old parents discussing their employment prospects.

These days it is not to submit. We are doomed if we do not make efforts. One of them expressed her views. The old man spoke rather in gloomy tones.

'I have to sit home. Being a man I should earn. But my eyes? I can hardly see . . .'

Sona protested 'No father. Do not wail. Old age is for every one of us. Why to discriminate between man and woman? Why should not we work? Why should not we earn?'

Rakhi supported her sister and patted her old father's shoulder. 'Why should you remind us we are girls? Why to use a different yardstick for girls? I say, let's give up different moral yardsticks for the two sexes. Society makes us docile and domesticated. Are we just dolls?' She displayed a lot of self-confidence. Her emotions were explicit on her face. Tears welled up in her eyes, perhaps a faint recollection of her dead brother.

Rajeev suddenly took hold of Smita's hand and looked deeply into her eyes before departing.

'I'll come to inform you.' He spoke with an emotion.

5

Rajeev's face was aglow with a deep-rooted sentiment. No disillusionment. There was no cynicism in his thinking. It, perhaps, comes only with advancing age. He must fight the total power system.

For the last two years he has been contesting college elections. He often told students that college unions are not meant to agitate students; to incite them to go on strikes. It is to help them in self-growth. He would often express himself to crowds of students. His opponents talked of something which students liked. 'Delay in examinations or their cancellations and no attendence. Maximum help in copying.' The students would go mad with clapping, whistling and thumping. Whenever Rajeev tried to protest, he was cowed down 'No body wants to listen to you. These things are of the past. These just don't carry any value whatsoever. If you don't keep shut, we would throw you.' Ajeet's closeones almost chanted a chorus. 'Don't give false hopes to your mates. What type of leaders are you? No responsibility!'

'Shame, Shame!'

Rajeev's voice would be lost somewhere in a deep valley of confused voices.

Ajeet would shout, 'Rajeev is crazy, mad and stupid. A *chumcha*, a dog . . .'

Then he would blast him, 'Rajeev, you just get lost, otherwise. I just can't control my supporters. Unruly consequences, not my fault. You see.'

More then once he was whished away from such gatherings.

It was the dead night when Ajeet and his accomplices had knocked at the door 'We have come with offers.' The second-in-command had spoken in no uncertain words.

'Accept them. Money, wine, woman . . . you can opt for all of them . . .'

It took him sometime to recognize the faces in darkness. The import of their visit did not immediately dawn on his sleepy nerves.

A feeble female voice struck their ears, 'Who is there? I say . . . who is there?'

'Mother . . . don't you mind. Continue sleeping. No worry . . . no problem.'

'I shall talk to you later on, Ajeet. Yes . . . in the morning in the college canteen.'

Rajeev almost pushed them away from his door-step.

A surging black silence was left behind with their departure. Rajeev stood mute at the door staring in vacancy. Shocked to the brim, he fell into a contemp-lative reverie. Leaders of tommorow! They will nourish the foundations? He felt dizzy.

People like Ajeet emerging as leaders!

He was confronted with a crumble, a crumble involving the entire built up of political system.

'Curious? he mumbled to himself. Others will follow him. The serious ones, the thinking ones. We can't measure up such situations. Quiet and aloof and right thinking people cut off and driven to the edge like standing water.'

The tranquil aspect of his thinking was thrown into a violent emotion. He was almost on the verge of a nervous break down. He walked into the interior of the house. His mother lay in the charpoy caught in the snatches of dozing.

'Who was at the door? At this time? No danger?' She uttered broken sentences. Her uttrances invariably sandwitched, 'No danger.' The oft repeated words indicated her mental sickness, a malady she had imbibed after the death of her husband.

She dozed off into a mumble of no meaning. Rajeev was left awake. All sorts of ideas entered and re-entered his sub-conscious. Rajeev was left awake. Should he withdraw from college elections? One is not objective and tranquil in some moments of one's life. What pained Rajeev most was the rejection of his right type of solutions to problems. His dis-illusionments were yet to have their sway. These came at a much later stage.

He must contest the elections. May be sanity prevails on some students in the college and he is able to win. His mind was criss-cross of conflicting ideas. Ajeet wanted him to withdraw.

The past stood like a looming reality before Rajeev's eyes playing many ups and downs in his psyche. Earlier he was not able to win elections but his fights did not go waste.

His presence in the college politics could not be dismissed as a riff-raff. It was positive. It was to reckon with. Most of us are rendered passive spectators. During elections Rajeev had his supporters but to Ajeet a lot of help came from unknown sources. They were beaten upon installing Ajeet as the President of the college union.

Morning shadows were already evident before Rajeev went to sleep.

6

Almost a week elapsed before Rajeev gave final touches to his determination regarding the pitching up a tent for fasting. To begin with, it could be a lonesome affair and might not attract much attention. He might meet a lot of opposition from his rival groups. These would not like to be exposed political connections. To them these were a cosy shelter for their way-ward desires and whims. They had already played havoc with public establishments. From time to time shop-keepers were pestered to yield money. It was done to create panic in the town. No resistance? Why? Shopkeepers always compromised on not very exorbitant sums of money.

They did not wish to be involved in any nuisance. Parting with little sums of money, they could buy their peace well and good. No harm. No use approaching the district authorities. They had their connections with them also. Moreover, Ajeet was adept at playing some tricks beyond the moral framework of Rajeev's working. Sooryakant remained the main stay to these miscreants giving all support. Odds to Rajeev's fasting were real. But he had faith in the earnestness of his purpose. May be he pricks the conscience of the people to make them realize their passivity. His thoughts travelled between the edges of the possible and the impossible. He consulted a few of his intimates also. 'It is not worth. People care a fig for such fasts. They have ways to demoralize you and throw you out of the tent.'

Tripathee, one of Rajeev's friend, spoke unhindered.

Scanning Rajeev's face he spoke in an assured manner, 'Most of us think fasts are humbugs. We even don't bother to look at the posters. They like to keep up their routine.

'But I have a cause . . . a commitment.' Rajeev stammered.

Public is self-centered, self occupied. No time for wider matters. Rajesh did not mince words. Rajeev went into a snappy contemplation.

'It could result in a grim fight. You know, Rajeev, Ajeet's group is determined. They have fought their battles on unfair grounds. Arn't you aware of their nefarious designs? They have been keeping the campus under a constant disturbance.'

"Quite-right. Tripathee, I don't disagree with you. But . . .'

'But . . . what?'

'Battles are always fought. We must land ourselves in the arena and not anticipate results.'

Rajeev was able to extract a half-hearted consent of his close-friends. Smita was there. She was a thinking sort. Moreover she would give him a lot of emotional feed-back.

It was partly a cloudy day. Clouds were not constant around the firmament of the sun. It was their game of see-saw with the brightest source of energy. Rajeev was there in a sequestered corner of the road-side. There were two helpers to put up a tent. Posters were pinned up with the rough exterior of the tent.

'Who are responsible for Krishna's death?'

'Expose the culprits.' Stand up for the conscience,' were some of the unusual words shining on the playcards. It was a humble shelter for the stray visitors. Permission had already been sought from the authorities. The day advanced with a steady progress of the activities of the day. The streets of the small town ran with rickshaw-pullers, carts, tongas and occasional buses. The roads stood dimlylit with poles often fitted with fused bulbs.

The town under description fifty years ago did not live with political fervour. It had its fascinating, tranquil aspects. People lived a life of steady pace. It was a contented, easy flow of life punctuated with handshakes and mutual saluations. Slowly the pace went off with the usual gear and took unwanted directions. Unlike fifty years ago landscape of human relations drifted towards neutral contours. Human warmth slowly trickled away with the coming up of new buildings.

'Why should I bother for him? He is None of our concern. Let him first oblige me.'

'Why should I greet them?' were some of the sentences alive like pricks in the sub-conscious flow of the town-folks. Further divides were the outcome of political electioneering.

The tent was pitched up in a frequented corner of the road. It was a part-yet aloof from the general hub-bub of the flow of the road. No obstruction was offered to the life of the town.

Rajeev, Tripathee, Smita and Rajesh were the four occupants of the tent. They were on their natural moods without betraying an iota of excitement. They might attract attention or their efforts may come to a naught.

Smita and Rajeev sat in the centre of the tent with playcards displayed around them.

'Yes . . . a long way to go . . .'

Passersby did not have time to look at them. Time trickled on with movement of needles on the surface of the clock. There ensued long spaces of silence.

'Why not to pray to God?' Smita beamed out with a suggestion.

'No harm . . .' Tripathee and Rajesh rejoined.

'It would add seriousness . . . atleast some kind of holyness to our mission.'

'Our cause is noble and pious. It's selfless. It involves the death of an innocent yougman.'

'Not only Krishna's death. What about those dying in the general spread of violence?'

They talked like intellectuals expressing their doubts and convictions.

'Violence and democracy, just opposed to each other. Some violent incidents are beyond our belief. Ghastly terror giving birth to situations.' Rajeev spoke in a subdued tone.

'Something definitely wrong with this land of Mahaveer and Buddha. The entire set-up is seething with hatred and callousness . . .'

'Newspapers are reporting but violence.'

'Seems to be traps of death . . .'

Their fasting continued throughout the day. It was in the evening that some students appeared in the tent. Their primary reaction was one of fun. They found Smita and Rajeev sitting side by side. It gave birth to a number of remarks.

'This is the best way to enjoy life. At least you two can sit together.'

For small town college students it was a matter of great diversion and curosity. Only boys were around.

'Rajeev, you might get a thrashing. You don't know people around. They might take an exception to it.'

A grave looking boy remarked.

The rest of the boys present in the tent looked around as if to trace some threads of romance going on in the tent.

'Better at home. Take her to some secluded place. Talk to her as much as you like, but to expose yourself and this girl to general public!'

'Scandolous!' The grave looking student continued in the manner of oratory. His well-worded piece of advice generated around a lot of giggling and then boisterous laughter. Rajeev was dumb-founded for a while. He had not anticipated this aspect of the present situation. He had thought his fasting would have moral impact. It would create ripples in the conscience of his mates in the college. The ugly aspects of the situation had not made their awareness in his thinking.

Smita was the only girl present in the tent. It might spread rumours in the town. And what about her family? O God! Rajeev was nervous and panicky. She seemed to be struggling with her own self. A fight within. She was bound to get a bad name. Her father was already a ruined figure. His maciated, hollowed eyes didn't show any trace of revival. His slow-fluttering eye-lids sometimes came to a stand-still giving to him the resemblance of a corpse. He might slip through the gate of death. Then she must pick-up courage. After all a fight has to be there. Life is a constant fight. Many eyes were concentrated upon her. Yes, she would be free from the blemish once her motives were surfaced.

She spoke in a high-pitched tone, 'Why should I go home? I say . . . Why? Am I doing something wrong, immoral? I'm on fast for a right cause.'

Her voice was firm and came out of the depth of conviction. The students around fluittered, swayed and showed their teeth in the most stupid manner.

'Jhansi-Ki-Rani . . .' 'Indra Gandhi' were the names associated with Smita. These were uttered more to ridicule than to admire this girl.

There were lights on the roadside heralding the night. Slowly the crowds would become thinner. Small town roads don't attract crowds during the night. Moreover there are movies to pin-them at homes. Thanks to television. Some stray students still sat in the tent. Smita's face was aglow with the possibility of the events may create highly inflammable situations. She might be led to a disaster of great magnitude. Even if some immoral heap is thrown over her, she would be free from the moral predicament once she announces her intention of marrying Rajeev. And that was for him to announce. She threw a compulsive glance at his face. He was tense, lost somewhere in the depth of his sub-conscious. It was a nerve-shattering moment for them. Smita was reluctant to look at Rajeev. She must maintain her neurtrality otherwise her emotion would betray her to the public exposure.

Students around are bent upon heaping a scandal on the present situation. And once a trace of scandal gets way, things would go beyond their precinits. Rajeev's mind was in a racy influx of ideas without any destination. He looked in front of him. There stood a wall of a crumbling structure at a visible distance from him. Adjacent to the wall stood a newly erected establishment lighted profously. Smita's anticipation came true when she found her father ambling towards her. He was followed by Sona and Rekha. There hung clouds of anger, doubt and anguish on the three faces. They came towards the tent with unsteady steps. There might be a lot of out-bursting and up-roar. Smita was determined not to budge and break her fast. Suddenly Gandhi's lean figure flashed in her sub-conscious giving a pip to her sagging spirits. Smita's father was nothing but anger at the moment, when he arrived in the tent.

'How dare you sit here, foolish girl? Aren't you a bit ashamed of yourself? After Krishna's death, you are serving a blow to the family.'

His words carried a lot of bittermess. Rekha was extremely aggressive in tune. 'You . . . a witch! You . . . the spoiler of our reputation. You are already the talk of the town. Our Mohalla talks nothing but your fasting with Rajeev. Is this the way to run your family?' Rekha's sharp tone was interrupted by Sona equally in a bad temper.

'And you Rajeev . . . was it for this you visit our home? You . . . a shameless boy! Will Krishna come back with your fasting? Why are you mum? You are guilty. Are you a well-wisher?'

Rekha's drawl of words remained unabated. 'What do you think? Are you in a big city? Foreign country? It is a small town. Here they know everything about everybody. Smita, you get up at once . . . otherwise we will drag you out of the tent.'

The curious group of a few students did not make any gesture of approval or disapproval. They sat still staring at the faces registering quick succession of all sorts of emotions. To them this family was intense and intriguing. It was a source of a lot of back-chat. Moreover it was free of cost. We need something to talk about. After all life without gossip is a big vaccum. The last blow was served by the old man which he pointedly spoke to Rajeev. 'And what do you think of yourself? Can you fight the *goondas*? You will be thrown away with your tent. Smita, you will get a bad name.' Rajeev and Smita were being hurled at curses and invectives. They were being condemned beyond their normal apprehensions. Then quiet discended upon their tense faces. Rajeev sat with his palm spread over his face. Rajeev must fed up some courage and spoke in a daring tone 'Baba, Gandhi got us freedom with fasting . . .' The old man's eye-lids made a movement. His face furrowed a bit and in a laughing tone he put in.

'Are you Gandhi? Rajeev . . .'

'No, no, no . . . I'm a bit of his follower. Truth, to begin with, is difficult to cope with but later on it shines brightly. It takes time. Think of Krishna's death. An innocent death. No one protests deaths of the innocents. It is a complete system we are protesting against. Don't you worry about Smita. No blemish will come to her. Rest assured . . .'

The old man's eyes blinked as he strained to grasp the full intent of Rajeev's rejoinder.

'I'll not let Smita get a bad name.' Rajeev's tone was firm and mysterious.

The oldman and the two sisters now showed a lesser intensity and tension. Their anger also took a down-ward trend.

Smita was a bit relaxed when she spoke to her sisters, 'Why, I can't understand my mistake? I'm in the tent for a cause. Is it immoral? Sisters, why do you look like this at me? Was not Krishna your brother also?'

There were instant tears in their eyes.

'True, true . . . but your sitting here, in the tent is objectionable. There is already a rumour in the Mohalla. They can't understand a girl sitting in the tent. This will create family problems. We might be . . .'

'Am l n't a human being . . . ?'

'Of course, you are Smita. But you are a girl. You need protection . . .'

Smita did not budge from her point of view. She held her resolve to continue fasting. The next day proved to be adverse to them. There were posters on walls involving Smita and Rajeev. The cause was lost somewhere behind the big posters. Who could have managed all this? Rajeev was on pins through out the day. Smita's apprehensions had taken a grim shape and reality. To whom should she explain her conduct and intention and there was none to listen. Her father might breathe his last. He would easily slip through the gate of death as there was hardly any trace of strength in him. Should she abandon all this? Should she retrace her steps and go back to her cell? The same routine . . . They might be thrown from the college. The principal might take a drastic step and throw her on the road side.

She fell racked beyond endurance.

'Rajeev, what should we do now? Gandhi seems to be failing us. He says truth wins in the long-run. Are we to be dismissed like this?' She spoke with tearful eyes. Her face betrayed an isolation leading to a delimma in her mind. Was there no way out? She constantly expressed her tense-grief.

'Don't worry Smita. May be clouds pass over with their black shadows!' Rajeev was almost in a state of mental consternation.

Rajesh and Tripathee sat mute; their faces buried in their palms. They must face consequences. The principal would not side with them. Rajeev knew his adversaries too well. He uttered in a prophetic tone, 'it's well calculated, deliberate and meant to shell-shock our present venture. Scandles are the easiest handle to terminate an agitation.' His words echoed in his depressed friends; Rajesh and Tripathee.

Tripathee so far had been in a philisophical mood contemplating the low morality to great causes. He was a boy of few words. Somehow he did not deserve Rajeev. In the riff-raff flow of life, some of them stick to their guns. It happens wth some of us. Tripathee was one of them. He looked at Rajeev and said, 'You should not have involved Smita. You see man-woman relationship is delicate in our society. Small towns pep-up scandles. Even the so-called broad-minded have a rot in their thinking. We have given the easiest handle to our enemies. You see . . . They have given the first mighty blow to our resolve to fight the inane . . .'

There was an obvious pall of gloom in the tent. The situation might take an ugly turn. The so-called protections of morality may up-root them, attack them and then demolish them.

'I fear a public-attack under the garb of morality. They think it's a boy-girl contrivance to be together.'

'But . . . but . . . we could be together at home also . . . at a hidden, convenient place. The very fact that we are together on the road-side is a proof of our innocence.'

Rajeev was a bit excited. His face displayed an innocent conviction. The sun stood just in front high in the sky spreading a lot of brightness.

Everything was exposed to its glare. There were obvious shadows of tension in the tent. Since morning no visitor had come there. At times imagination takes to distorted forms leading us to contemplate the sinister, un-pleasant. The inmates were led to believe that they were being isolated from the general flow of humanity. A sort of gulf existed between the two. It does not take much time to spread ill news in a small town. Moreover posters carying their names . . . ! Yes . . . they have lost public sympathy. No one is interested n them and their cause.

Rajeev was quite tense. He looked at Smita. She too was lost in a maze of thinking.

'Ruin leads to ruin. Krishna gone for ever. Father too old to support the family. And now the reputation of the family gone to dogs.'

There seemed to be the play of glimmer of darkness and the sun-shine before her eyes. She was in a very isolated dejection.

'May be Sona and Rekha go unmarried. Its because of me. Society punishes bold girls. They want them to be polite and dogmatic. Just born for a rotten routine. Once she steps out, there is a lot of hue and cry. A lot of resentment . . .'

Her words were drowned in the din of a big group of students coming to them. All of them seemed to be in a mood of half-violence. A mob has a flow, a fluidity. It may take any road convenient to it. This unruly group must be faced otherwise the cause is lost for ever. A zig-zag crowd of students flanked the tent. It followed a lot of sneering, swearing, moping and unwanted gesturing.

'Majnoo and Lailla . . . But they are modern.'

'No, no . . . they are fighting for a cause. With posters around the town.'

There was a clap-trap and giggling.

'Take away the tent. *Badmaash.* Slurring the town and college . . .'

Meanwhile Rajeev, Smita, Rajesh and Tripathee were on their feet. They stood like rocks to encounter the flow of the unruly students.

'Morality-posers . . . Enjoying with a girl . . .'

'Shut up . . .' Rajeev's voice was tremulous, vibrant and piercing.

'Oye . . . hero . . . Don't shout . . . Filmi hero . . . the princpal has already expelled you from the college. See the Notice-Board.'

'Go away . . . Vacate the tent. Otherwise . . . the police may arrest you.'

Some of them gave a violent shaking to the tent.

'Don't touch it. What is our fault?'

'You are spreading scandle . . .'

'Not we . . . they are spreading.'

'Who are they?'

'They know . . . they know it well. Listen to me . . .' Rajeev regained his breath. 'Why should we come to road-side to create a scandle? Scandles are done at hidden places. Not on the road-side. Why should we expose ourselves to public? I say, try to understand. People don't bring romances or scandles to the public view. They hide it. Yes, they keep it a secret. They hood-wink others. But we are in front of you. Are we ignorant, stupid to advertise our relationship?'

Rajeev's voice was solid, determined and carried a lot of heart-stirring emotion. He boldly looked at their faces.

Another voice. Tripathee's voice came out of thickly shourded lips 'Don't misunderstand us. We are of you . . . your own friends. Posters on walls are to discourage us, to wind up our tent. You don't know, we have enemies. Your ememies . . .'

The quientened crowds stirred up 'who are they? Let's know, Let's know.'

'I can't tell you just now. I wouldn't . . . but . . . they are afraid to be exposed. Those responsible for the ruin of the town.'

The mob was contained. It proceeded towards emotional, logical conclusions. Some of them still retained their irresponsible zest towards the situation. To them it was a matter of great joy and excitement. All sorts of students could not be tamed mentally, could not be brought to holy stage of mind to which Rajeev was leading them. They had been participating in mob-type situations in strikes. Some of them had made a nuisance of themselves in classes. They had not anticipated that there could be an agitation with a lot of seriousness.

Some of them expressed themselves in negative tones.

'Rajeev is a defeated candidate, when he couldn't win a college election, he can't win in this battle. It's a bigger battle.'

'He'll be arrested. I heard some people talking. They say . . . the Government will not allow this non-sense.'

A big boy with tiny eyes in his sockets kept starring at the fasting couple. His stare carried an angry complexion-dim traces of mockery.

'You are already expelled from the college . . . both of you. Why . . . I learn Rajesh and Tripathee are also in the hit-list.'

The big, mainly voice rolled and sounded like a drum. He did not look like a student. His bearing was of an outsider or someone deployed to carry out nefarious orders. His bulging eye-lids gave the impression of an impish look, 'I heard the principle saying that he is ready to take you back on the college—roll if you quickly windup . . .'

'By the way. Who are you? We have never seen you on the college premises. An outsider?'

He took two minutes in framing an answer. 'No . . . no . . . not an outsider. Insider. Very much an insider. But I'm your well-wisher. Better wind-up and depart.'

The dialogue between the two had already caught their attention. It offered the possibilities of a grim wordy war-fare.

'Better keep the piece of advice to yourself.' Rajeev spoke in a stern voice.

'Mind your tone. I am not used to such tones, what is this you are fighting for? Your principles!' His mocking tone caricatured the present situation worthy of a quick dismissal.

Rajeev took his eyes off the blackish face and became attentive to some of the students in the crowd.

'My fault? Let me know my fault. Am I fighting for promotion? Some selfish end? You think and reply. Was not Krishna of the town? Building razed to ashes. I would not be sold with any price. That's my promise. Then why don't you stand by me? Point a finger at my fault, my selfishness, I'll abandon it. I have no money. I don't offer drinks to my supporters. I'm. I'm.'

His tears rolled down his lanky cheeks. He mumbled rest of the words without looking at them.

Rajesh came out with words cohering into a sort of ceremonial statement 'Yes . . . that's true. Before joining him, We searched his mind and soul. Questioned him. Interogated him. He is innocent. Pledge to be with him. Make up your mind. Think at home.'

The big manly voice was thrown in a rear. There emerged a sort of zest in the mob. It was a sort of emotional pick-up natural among the youth. They seemed to be in a psychological conflict. At least they could not dismiss the present situation, a mere scandle. There was a lot of brain-searching. Commoners do respond to logic, once they understand it. The tide seemed to flow in the opposite direction. Situations have to be fought. But it was not the end of Rajeev's tribulations.

'Rajeev, we are with you. Ask for any help. Krishna's death. Yes, we remember.'

A faint sound flickered in the crowd like ripples in a tank.

The big manly voice seemed to be suffering from isolation. It was getting cornered, so it departed unnoticed.

Rajeev stood up erect and spoke in mild tunes, 'we must tear off posters from the walls. It is a cooked up story for me and Smita. Just to malign us. Slur upon us is calculated and deliberate. It's a wipe out of our present agitation.'

Rajeev could vividly make out the effect of his words on the students around him. They were moved and ready to tear off posters. He was quiet for a few minutes and then again picked up his flow of words. 'Why can't a girl go on fast? In big cities, they don't mind all this. What is immoral about it? Tell me. Is Smita not a part of humanity? She is a human being like any one of us. Moreover Krishna was her real brother. Wasn't he? Can't a sister express her sorrow on the death of her brother? I say, speak to me.'

Rajeev spoke with an intense emotion. He seemed to be inspired by some unseen force coming to his rescue. At times he had errie awareness of unseen forces. These must be somewhere behind the visible. After all life is not all matter. There are heightened moments, Consciousness leading us towards evolution. These moments are rare and precious. A retreating tide of his feelings swept him towards a shadowy Sooryakant. His sinister presence in his sub-conscious made him shaky. This man would do anything to establish his political identity. And what about Ajeet? He has not been to the tent even once. Why? Ajeet and his friends are fully aware of his fasting. May be the boy with big voice was deputed by them? He was on an errand. There was no doubt, otherwise he should not have come here. He broke his contemplation for a while to find the departure of all students from the scene.

Smita broke her silence.

'Rajeev, you go absent-minded. What does trouble you? You did not notice even the departure of the crowd. They wanted to talk to you, but . . .'

'Really?'

'Am I talking to no purpose?'

'I mean . . . you . . . see, it looks so odd.'

'Really?'

'Tripathee . . . O God! Really . . . really . . .'

'Are you off your wits Rajeev?' There was a big laughter. It was perhaps to ward off the tension that had accumulated around them following unexpected situations.'

Smita was less tense resulting in brightness over her face. Her face became more expressive. She stole a bright glance at Rajeev. Their eyes met for a while synthesizing the chemistry of their brains. An intense moment stolen out of the dull influx of routine! What a relief? It was mere than more emotional refreshment. It was sport of a peculiar kind of joy tending towards sublimity. Smita's tone carried a lot of gaiety. Thank God. Posters will be off the town-walls. I say . . . Rajeev . . . in fact, these posters are of no harm to us personally because . . .'

'Well-well . . . personally these are O.K. What about our movement and fasting?'

'Posters will definitely create a bad impression upon the general public.' Rajesh spoke with a lot of grimness.

'We can't afford to be complacent.'

'Expect an attack at any moment.'

'They will not rest unless we are up-rooted.'

'Why? Who?' Smita's questiions came in an unwarranted way.

'It is as simple as day light. We have powerful enemies in those we are trying to expose. Don't think they want us to continue. Krishna's death is not an isolated incident. It's connected with people. These indulging in the politics of crime, violence, dishonesty and whatn't?' Tripathee couldn't contain himself. 'Such groups are scattered all over the country. To them crime and poiltics are the real aspects of the game. End is to be achieved, means are not important. It was for nothing Bapu gave a tinge of morality to politics. Ends and means both pure and holy.'

Rajeev let out a deep sigh with his utterance.

We have come to such a pass. A state of affairs leading us to a moral chaos. Society begins to crumble once sanctity is divorced from politics.

Today nothing is right. Protests, stokes without moral implications. Without any commitment. They are these just like that. Some of them in holidaying mood or on purchasing spree.

And most of them are either bought or brought to movements.

There was an abrupt ceassion of discussion.

Some people strayed in the tent. Clad in spotless white, they gave the impression of being social workers. The prominent among them had an air of authority about him. He gave the impression of being offended at what was going on in the tent.

His lips twitched in a peculiar shape and eye-lids narrowed before he addressed himself to the occupants of the tent, 'I am well-known at least in this state. All of them know me. I mean the chiefminister, ministers and all prominent leaders of the state. I am called Sahaya.'

He proffered his hand to Rajeev. Expectancy sat on their faces. Sahaya demanded a glass of water and then he began in an advisory tone, 'You are students. Your primary aim is to study books. Then why should you sit here wasting your time?' None of them spoke anything and then the same voice was heard. 'Politics is not any easy job these days. Tell me what do you want? Compensation to Krishna's death? But it has already been paid.'

Rajeev was amazed, 'How do you know about all this? Curious! Mr. Sahay how do you know?'

He let out a short giggle before speaking. 'How do I know? Why? I know almost everything about the state. Yes, almost everything concerning strikes.'

He imparted a massive twinkling to his eye-lids. His lips quivered to express something but stayed back for a while. And then he picked up his tone coming out like a ritual, 'That's a part of my assignment. After all strikes are an important aspect of our national life. So I am mindful of them.'

Rajeev was impressed a lot by whatever the new arrival spoke to him.

'You must be discriminating in stikes, fasting and *Dharnas*. In fact we should undertake such steps for the welfare of the common people. To some noble aim . . .'

'Noble aim?' The leader of the three persons responded at once 'what is the noble cause you are fighting for? Suppose to come to lime-light. To bag a ticket in the coming elections.'

Rajeev and his intimates were shocked beyond surface reaction. This aspect of the situation had never occured to them.

Tripathee was a bit furious, 'what do you mean Mr. Sahaya? We have no political ambition. It is to expose those connected with Krishna's death. Those connected with the destruction of the town.'

Sahaya, Gandhi and Sharma started laughing. One of them spoke, 'You see causes are always noble, only high achievements are personal.'

'Anyway . . . Are you willing to sell this agitation to us?'

'Sell . . . ? I don't understand.' Rajeev felt dumb-founded.

'You see . . . its as clear as the sun-shine. You sell the agitation to us. Then we will see . . .'

'Are you a professional agitator?'

'Exactly, Now you understand us better. We are always ready to join any agitation. But what's the use?'

These revelations before them were beyond their belief. Selling an agitation? Profits?

'Democracy, values, real protest all gone to dogs. O God! What a moral vaccum!'

'What are you thinking Mr. Rajeev?'

'Brilliant offer for you. Back out of it! Get away with a lot of money. They pay lip service to martyrs. Consult your friends, I think this girl will guide you properly. Girls are more practical and down to the earth.'

Rajeev and his friends were shaken beyond measure. They didn't know how to extricate themselves from the situation created by Sahaya. Yet they maintained their exteriors. It was second blow to that deep rooted convictions and ideals. Their struggle, reduced to currency notes!

Adolescent minds are sensitive to some issues. They feel more than the grown ups. Moreover their feelings are raw and are attuned to some ideals.

'I know what is passing on in your mind Mr. Rajeev. We understand your feelings. Days for ideal agitations are gone.' Sharma's tone was firm.

'I know . . . we are shocking you but the reality remains unchanged. You stand benefitted if you pass on the agitation to us.'

Sahaya was desperate with his words. By the time many students came there. They were rather breathless.

'No poster in the town. The job is done. The leading one gasped for words.'

'Well-done! Well-done!'

'It does'nt take much time to revive the posters.' Sahaya gave out a brief chuckle.

'You opponents are not small flies. Big fights ahead. That's why. But that time more students collected in the vicinity.'

'O.K. We leave. Think over it, Our offer stands. You can't manage this job. You don't have the resources.'

They were ready for departure.

'We shall come again. Mr. Rajeev. May be by that time you grow maturer and realistic.'

Sahaya, Gandhi and Sharma made leader like greetings, salutations and left the tent. Rajeev and his co-mates were left in a strange kind of disillusionment. This is how most of the agitations make their way. Most of them are mechanical and bereft of real ideal stuff. They had a queer sense of loss within their psyche and their inner ponderings were nothing but waves of self-depreciation.

Smita's mind wondered in the era of struggle for freedom. The entire country was under the sway of feelings of sacrifice, idealism and patriotism. She imagined hordes of people fighting against the Raj. It was a fight to something impersonal and something outside them. To them, the country was the real object to be identified with. How could they undergo tortures and untold punishments? Wherein lay the ignition point? Smita was almost talking to herself. Rajeev discerned the stuggle within her.

'I say, you have gone silent after their departure. Aren't you perturbed Smita?'

'Yes, Yes. I'm being driven to the Father of the Nation. I wonder how could he onspire sacrifice, confidence in the hearts of millions? The illiterate, suffering and the downtrodden became the backbone of the country. He never compromised his ideals, he was stead-fast and truly dedicated.'

'But there must have been some force governing his activities.'

'Yes, the force of morality and his conscience. Moreover he fully identified himself with the cause of the down-trodden. He did not carved out isolation for himself preaching inane ideals.' Rajeev's voice was a bit emotional colouring his inner landscape. A group of students stood listening to what Rajeev was speaking.

'Mere idealism and telling ideals to others does not matter. To drive an ideal one must practice it. One must identify one self with the ideal.'

His tone took a deeper emotional fervour.

'You see, human beings crave for the achievement of some ideals. They can't live in a vaccum. There must be somthing higher for our striving.'

One of students present in the tent got impatient with Rajeev's high-sounding views. He abruptly stopped Rajeev. 'you speak too much. You have not bothered to enquire about the story of posters.'

'What is there to talk about them?'

'Already off form the walls.'

'One for the time being.'

'You fear too much.'

'No, you are proving to be a simpleton.'

'You perhaps know posters were put up by a groups of *Goondas*.'

'True . . .'

'They may repeat . . . , Everthing is fair in love and war.'

'So?' He questioned in a tone of anxiety.

'You must depute students on vigil.'

'There can be violence also.'

'Yes, we are aware. In that case we must be alert.'

'The police, the administration are with them.'

'Can't the innocent and feelingful people run agitations in the country?'

'You always stray in the lanes of idealism Rajeev. That's the basic weakness with you.'

The remark was from a short statured, flat-nosed boy. His eyes stood deep in the sockets blinking at him like the weak joints of an electric bulb. Rajeev was a bit appalled at his remark. Can an ordinary student understand all this? He always underestimated others. They also have their eyes and ears.

Rajeev made him sit near him and enquired about his parents and the class in which he was studying.

'How you know about me, Mohan?'

'Why? It's so simple. At our age we are full of idealism and enthusiasm. But . . .'

'But what . . . ?'

'But crime and foul means have their impact on our process of electioneering. You want prominence.'

'But I am not in for prominence . . .'

The day passed off without any significant event in the tent.

41

7

The night was unusually dark throwing a dense pall over the small town. Electricity poles were also blinded. Life seemed to be disappearing from the narrow roads and by-lane shops were closed. Rajeev's tent stood like a ghost in the nearly deserted streets. Rajeev was not relaxed and Smita was under the spell of a powerful depression. They have already undergone a lot of fear of the unexpected chain of events. Anything sinister might ensue resulting in a big disaster in their lives. There have been moods of depression, ponderings. Should they retrace their present predicament? How cumbersome to face uncertainties? Perhaps only stocks are able to surmount these unhappy situations? Smita was lost in strange phobias leading her thoughts to frustrations and unhappiness. She felt the presence of two, big sinister eyes keeping an unhealthy vigil over their activities. There wasn't much of mention of their fasting in the town. Her tensionbrimmed mind no longer could contain her tears.

'We have thrown ourselves in a very intricate situation. There seems to be no respite to my fears.'

Rajeev put up a face of boldness. 'Don't worry. In the beginning things look bad . . . but then they look better.'

'But when?'

Their conversation found echoes in Tripathee and Rajesh also. 'How long? How long can we go on fasting without any attention?'

'Results?'

The night was on its way to advancement. Some moments become tense with a conglomeration of nagging ideas and situations. Their words were reduced to whispers. It's a fight within and a fight without against a blurring situation. There swam a pall of fear among the four inmates of the tent. Perhaps the unconscious travels in the remotest, darkest lanes of the inner resesses of the human psyche. There was a lot of darkness in the sky-like a canopy misshapen. There were foot steps hurrying towards them. Fear stricken they made an attempt to pierce the darkness around them. Yes, they were three-four of them with their faces covered with clothes. Their only aim was to kidnap Smita and then create panic in the town. They pounched upon her like vultures without tearing away her flesh. The attack was abrupt, quick and well-planned. They did not allow her to shriek or give any indication of protest.

Rajeev was crucially hit on his head rendering him incapable of offering an resistance. Tripathee and Rajesh were also spanked, thrashed and given heavy blows on their faces. They reeled, spun around and were flat on the ground. There was none to rescue them at the dead of night. A maruti van rushed out of the town carrying away Smita and her kidnappers. She was too dazed to judge her present situation. The operation was sleek, manipulated by trained hands.

'We wouldn't harm you physically in any way.' One of them peeped through the bandaged cloth over his eyes. His face was not completely explicit to Smita.

'Rest assured Smita sister. Our plan is to demolish your fasting and dismantle the tent.' Smita gained a lot of confidence when she heard of his assurance. The van was rushing on the paved roads and then taking *Kachcha* paths. It received a number of jolts on the mazy *Kachcha* path. Smita felt like shrieking at the prospect of encountering a hostile situation. Everything gone to dogs! Her honour in the town travels with a lot of blemish. They would think of all sorts of situations for us. Morality is likely to swim in the small town. Her name being repeated on the lips of towns-men! O God! Suddenly her family faces swam across her eyes. Sona, Rekha must find themselves in wilderness leading them to all types of situations and speculations. What will happen? She was tense with grief.

'But what? But what?' Her doubtfull thoughts seemed to be searching an anchor. The van moved to a place of isolation.

'Sure. Sure. We can even allow you to go back if you give up the seat of fasting. Persuade Rajeev.'

The van stopped and they came down. She was ushered in a room under the open horizons of the sky. The height was declining towards morning. Partial darkness enveloped the surrounding areas.

Smita looked around and was struk with an air of familiarity. Ajeet was there—the arch enemy of the agitational situation.

She almost pounched upon him sending him to shreds. 'Ajeet, I can't believe. It this the way to behave with college-mates?'

He sent forth a mild giggle.

'If you can stay with Rajeev so long, Why not with me for a few days? Any difference between me and Rajeev.'

'Shut-up Rajeev.'

'Suppose I take you to your parents. In that case I am a better person than Rajeev. He has put you in a very awkward situation. I plan to restore the dignity of your family. Smita dear, though you always voted against me.'

'Is that the cause for kidnapping me? Are you that petty, Ajeet?'

'Oh, no. That was just by the way. I mention. At the moment I'm connected with a big cause in my life.'

'What's that?'

'Rajeev and you must stop this agitation. It is against the peace of the town. It has already brought discontent among people . . . you . . . see.'

'But we are agitating for a cause . . .'

'For example . . .'

'There is a system that sends the innocent to death. There are people behind such happenings. Ajeet . . . You have become a criminal. As a student you have entered unwanted areas of life.'

'Politics is not unwanted. Without politicians we can't run the country.'

'True . . . true . . . absolutely true. Is it politics to get a girl of your college kidnapped by ruffians? Is it politics to destroy public property?'

Indeed Ajeet uttered the words in a jiffy and then left his seat. Smita was now free from all traces of fears and apprehensions, Atleast she has been transported among the known persons. No harm would come to her. But what? There may come a lot of harm to him. Her name has already appeared in many newspapers. She is the talk of the town. It might serve a deadly blow to her father. He might not be able to bear the shock. And she was morally upset. She can talk to Ajeet. But they wouldn't believe her. The society has different yard sticks for male and female morality. A fallen female is curse to her parents and to the society. What could she do? She should not have consented to go on fast with Rajeev. But Rajeev is dear to her. Very . . . Very . . . dear . . . her future life partner. He will accept her. She knows him too well. He knows this is a part of their struggle. For the first time the flow of consciousness had a bit of relaxation. She looked around the room intently to discover her situation in the room. Chairs and tables thrown in a zig-zag manner. The morning sun will illuminate many more things to her. There they were the main operators of the upheavels in the town.

She fell into a mood of past rumination. Last year this group had crossed all decent behaviour and had created a lot of panic in the town who does shelter them? There was a lot of hue and cry among the people of the town but their activities were given unbriddled directions. Their main victims used to be shopkeepers giving money in the name of agitations. The group would threaten them with all sorts of tricks. Curiously enough, the police stood passive spectators to the entire sequence of events. Without giving them any warning. Political patronage? Smita was now trying to probe the springs of their power.

Ajeet was now back with two cups of tea. He offered one of them to Smita and spoke in a lingering tone.

'See the difference between me and Rajeev. He seperated you from your family. To lead a poor girl to politics! I doubt his intentions about you. He is there to demolish you. No one will marry you and your sisters.'

Ajeet was at the top of his persuation to her, 'Girls are meant for homes.'

'But now I am out of it.'

'Your marriage prospects. Almost nill.'

'I wouldn't marry at all. Is it that necessary?'

'Then?'

'Then . . . I'll be active in politics.'

'You are a book worm. Hell of difference Smita. It is one thing to read books and quite another to turn to politics. Can you manage all what we are doing?'

'Suppose politics is far. With a tinge of morality.'

'You are no better than Rajeev. Chips of the same block.' He emitted peals of laughter rising in a crescendo.

'Any way. Our purpose is served. We have broken the back-bone of your fasting.'

'I doubt. But why don't you allow a common man to protest.'

'Protest is the job of a politician and not of a common man.'

'Why? Commoners also have something to protest against. Why only a politician?'

'He adds weight to political agitations. He is experienced. He knows how to give directions. Moreover it is whole time job. O, Yes . . . Yes . . .' Ajeet chuckled to himself.

'Rajeev. once told me your teacher episode.'

Smita tried to unnerve him. But it emboldened him.

'See Smita, that was just a beginning, a nice beginning, an appropriate beginning . . . The country is doomed . . .'

Smita looked at Ajeet placing the empty cup on the table.

'And now, when do you reach home?'

'That's my job. The only condition is, you will say, I saved you. O.K. No contrary statement, otherwise . . .'

'Otherwise . . .' Smita asked without a pother to his challenging tone.

'You know . . . my dare-devil deals. I can . . . yes . . . I can do a lot of harm.'

Smita thought it wise to be quiet for sometime. There are occasions when silence serves the purpose. She suddenly changed her attitude towards Ajeet. Her intent looking at Ajeet had a tinge of emotion and softness.

'You are bold indeed Ajeet. This I always kept on telling Rajeev. At least you can accomplish things. Only you could win elections, Rajeev couldn't.'

Ajeet felt quite pampered and excited about this new development. There was a flush on his face and he grew tender towards Smita.

'Whenever I visited your place, it was . . .' He suddenly stopped and looked at her.

'I can't express. You see. Rajeev did and . . .'

And then he gave a new direction to his argument, 'Rajeev seeks shelter in you. Solace, strength, What a psychology! And I'm ready to give you shelter. I wouldn't depend upon you. I'll give you protection. My future is also bright. Very bright.'

Smita was dazed for a while. She had never given a thought to this kind of relationship with him. He was one among the many of course, leading and prominent in the town. He could lead, contrive and achieve. Achieve what? Achieve destruction and perversion. Perhaps perversion is a prominent element in human nature. Her thoughts ran like unbridled horses, galloping . . . raising a lot of dust. She thought of exploiting his weakness for her.

'Ajeet, For whom? I mean, who does make you work?'

'Smita . . . I'm not that innocent. I have been in the profession for the last many years.'

'Professional?' Smita's lips parted in a strange amazement.

'Yes . . . it's a profession for me. I do my job and get money.'

'Who does give you money?'

'Again the same probing. Such important issues are disclosed among confidents. First you give up Rajeev and join us. We'll accomodate you. We need a girl like you. You are not the domestic type.

'You can launch out. Why? You are already in the areas. I'll get you a lot of money. No problem to your people. Otherwise, you carry your wretched existence.'

For the first time she was thrown into active ponderings. Ajeet withdrew with parting sentences. 'Think over it and then decide. You have already seen a part of our working. More will come to you in case you join our clan.

'I can't promise you forthwith. Let me think at home. There I feel more free and calm. It's a vital decision. First of all you should transport me home.'

'O.K. O.K. Smita.' Ajeet replied in the manner of a political gangster.

The dawn of the day light made Smita more conscious of her surroundings. Her room lay in the middle of a field. Her room was not well-maintained. A corner of the room was stuffed with empty bottles and a lot of unwanted stuff. She tried to recognize her kidnappers. They must be here around. It might be their deliberate planning on their part. They must have planned like this. They were not afraid of being arrested. She kept her surmises active and made her full efforts to act like a detective. Ajeet has to be fought. He is misled and being used by someone. The placid morning gave to her a lot of emotional soothing and tranquility. She pondered over the past night. What a turnout? A great moment of surprise! She anticipated the worst fortune for her. But it did not come out like that. A complete anticipation of future is not possible. That's what makes it future. She peeped outside through the window. Distant tall trees were yet to receive the glimmer of the morning sun. The horizons lay bare and peaceful A gentle breeze touched the tips of the standing crops putting them into a slow motion. The entire landscape within the vicinity of the brick-structure was caught up in to and fro movement. She felt a mild thrill. Rajeev must be anxous about her. Nascent experiences are rich experiences. Their sway is always sweeping. An experience that goes beyond expressions. With Rajeev she has a mental affinity. Both of them belong to lower-middle class families. They have to struggle together not only for their happy future but for certain issues that have thrown them into unison.

'Smita dear . . .' the address startled her but she offered no resistance.

'Let's go . . . the transport is there beyond the field. Let it be a quiet affair. Don't talk much about it. In that case I wouldn't be soft with you. I'll not enter your house. I'll drop you at the crossing. Then you can manage. There is no use going to the police against us.'

Smita kept on looking at Ajeet. Her mind was alive with questions. Only time will solve her riddles.

'By the way . . . why this drama of the past night?'

'Must I repeat? It was to demoralize you. To puncture your political ambitions.'

Smita was much surprised.

'Rajeev has them. He wishes to be on the forefront. Only he does not speak it out.'

8

The vehicle followed a comparatively obscure path. Before getting down the path, Smita thanked Ajeet profously and he reminded her of his proposal to her. Smita crept into the house without much noise and went straight into her room. She didn't want to invite the attention of the people of the lane.

But in the morning Smita was surrounded by women and men with all sorts of questions. Most of the questions were born out of cunningness and to explore the unhealthy situations of her present predicament.

'Where have you been? Taken away? By whom?' Her father was breathless as he embraced her time and again. Sona and Rekha were on the verge of weeping. Their mother was alreay in tears. They hardly spoke anything.

'Rajeev has been here. He is very sad. He wants to fight his enemies.'

'That problem we'll take up later on.' Smita said quietly.' No harm is done to me. I'm safe and sound. Don't worry. It's part of the game.'

'What about fasting?'

'Rajeev continues with it. He says he wouldn't give it up.'

There were foot steps in the room. Ladies of the lanes were there. Their faces hung with pretended grief were seen inside the room. Their eyes glued to Smita's face were trying to read the content of the happenings.

'Beti, we did not sleep the whole night. Your face kept on rushing to us. Who were they? What did they do?'

'What do you mean? Chachi, I was ready to kill myself if . . .'

'Ram, Ram. God has protected you Beti . . .'

'Yes, I'm safe and sound. I know how to deal with such people. I know it chachi.'

Smita blurted out her statement with a tinge of excitement.

'Were you afraid?' The enquiry was made by a woman without any teeth.

'Any girl will be afraid. Yes, I was afraid. They were four in van. Their faces were hidden under layers of cloth-pieces.'

'What did they do to you?'

'They behaved properly. They told me it was to harm the fasting. No other motive.'

One of the women was growing restless. She was pining to blurt her mind to this girl. 'You are a girl. Beti these are dirty people. Don't go to the tent. It does not suit a girl.'

'But . . . why . . . why not? We must fight. Women can do a lot. You seldom read newspaper full of women and their exploits. You are ignorant. Quite ignorant. You have spent your lives within the four walls of the house producing children and nothing else.'

Her tone carried fits of irritation and anger. Thoughtless creatures. But it was not their fault. They have been without books.

'Go. go. chachi. I'm tired. I'll talk to you later on. I'm tired.' Smita managed to send the group out of the home. No use discussing with these people.

Smita's home in the evening was subdued and mild. The rooms were partially lit because of the weak supply of electricity.

The day was dead and gone leaving frayed emotions. The town was comparatively quieter with a recession of pedestrains and vehicles. Smita came out of her room. Some women of the lane were around her mother. They kept themselves away from Smita because of the rough exterior she had presented to the lane women in the afternoon.

There was a mild spurt at the door as if pushed apart by two hands. The push was mild but heavy with the arrival of Rajesh and Tripathee. Tripathee walked straight to Smita and said, 'Come along. Rajeev wishes to talk to you. We are almost cured of the hurt. A mild ache is left in the body. The rest is O.K. You are O.K. I know you are a brave girl.'

Smita gave a mild approval to him with a nod.

'We were anxious, tense and full of the un-expected. We pondered over the possibilities with a lot of conjecturing. There is a limit to human supposition.'

'Who were they?'

'You know them. Ajeet and his clan.'

'O God, Ajeet? He knows you too well. Did he misbehave with you?'

'No. It wasn't nothing of the sort. But it was nerve shattering. I was exposed to all sorts of sinister possibilities, I could be. To think of that is simple, pure agony, torture beyond endurance.'

Smita was quietened and seemed to be fighting with her inner self. She was not inclined to expose her anguish to the public. It does not pay. It means invitation to all sorts of problems without much help.

'Rajeev can't leave the tent. Dismay and un-certainty in his thinking. He says . . .' Tripathee was breathless with expressions.

'Please . . . don't talk out internal matters here. For delicate matters tent is the best place. I'll come, Tell Rajeev . . . I'll come.' Smita bade them goodbye and rushed towards her room. Once one launches out one has to face problems. A beginning was made. Her future was uncertain. Her own people are against her. Only Rajeev understands her, loves her and they are made of the same clay.

Her mother talked to her, 'Beti, you must leave all this. We can't afford it.'

Smita didn't wish to draw the mother and the father into anguish. She wanted them to relax so she deferred her announcement of going to the tent.

'O.K. O.K. mother. I'll follow what you say.' It was uttered in low voice. It was more to appease the mother than to undertake any pledge of not joining the fast.

The moon hung in the sky like an orphan at the threshold of a house. Smita was in a state of turmoil. But! she must proceed. She has already brought a moral calamity to her household life. There is the life of instinct and there is the life of social taboos. The conflict is eternal. It creates ripples. It creates stirring in the minds of people and then a big whirlwind. She went to her father and touched his feet and spoke in suppressed sobs—'Father, you must allow me to go back to my fasting. It has to be carried on. It is a challenge. I know, you don't like it. You want me to live a domestic creature. May be later on I live like this. But at the moment, we are determined. Fight we must, our path is different.'

The father was too old to protest. His blinking eyes even could not capture the entire content of his daughter's words. He nodded implicitly. It was hardly expressive of anything. Sona and Rekha were in a mood to raise wild protest but spoke in mild tones, 'After Krishna's death, you are the biggest calamity on us. You have turned everything upside down. Quick happenings. Nothing is settled. You see, We do not know how to pull on. Our lives are ruined. What will you get out of this fasting? They wouldn't listen. Do they listen to folk like us?'

Sona was relentless in her expressions. Rekha was in full support to her views but was not restrained.

'It's not a situation of my making. Since I'm caught. I wouldn't leave. I'll try to manage for you.'

She hurriedly left her house in the dark of the night. Most probably she wanted to go unnoticed. She had a morbid dread of the staring eyes. A great sense of guilt clutched her as she felt that she was going too far. She walked down the narrow-lanes overwhelmed. Rajeev said, 'you are no longer the girl of four walls?' He got up to welcome her. His emotion was kept at bay like slashing waves near the sea-coast. He made her sit near him and put his searching eyes on her face, 'I know through bits the entire sequence of the attack on us. By the way who was the architect of the happening.'

'Your main rival, Ajeet. But he didn't mistreat me. He wished me to join his clan, why, I do't know. He didn't explain. He works for some one. I don't know. They are out to do mischief. Beyond all doubts. You follow . . .'

'Any news.'

'A lot of commotion in the town. People are no longer passive spectators, some of them visited us yesterday. They want us to shut. They say that the tent is the scandle point. Since you ask them to bring the culprits to law'

'Yes, they say. We are the culprits. We are fighting for nothing.'

'How to convince them?'

'I don't know. How to put new life into our agitation? How to draw people to us? They think we are just riff-raff without any serious aim. They think we are fighting for our own selfish motive.'

Smita and Rajeev, for the first time, had become conscious about the moral implications of the stir. Tripathee and Rajesh were also puzzled. An agitation without popular support does not last long. It dies its own death. All sorts of ideas raced their minds. Ajeet's group was bent upon demolishing them at any cost.

There lay a thick wall of darkness on distant contours of the town. The small town slept peacefully in the last phase of the night's journey across the vast globe. But for the illumination contrived by human dexterity, it was the reign of native darkness. Smita and Rajeev sat in the close vicinity of each other. Tripathee and Rajesh were dozng off in the corner of the tent. It was a snatch offer to the couple in the dead silence of the night. In the tumble and nose of the routine, we forget the existence of emotions. Perhaps their simmer is bedimmed under heavy burden of externals. But they are always there in the subtlest forms of planning in the sub-conscious lanes of human psyche. Smita peered at Rajeev with a lot of love concentrated in her eye-lids. Rajeev was alive to this human situation. He went near her, touched her face, eye-lids, 'Smita, I went almost crazy the night you were kidnapped. All sorts of distorted versions of the situation came to me. My little universe lay crumbling. I couldn't express. To whom could I explain.'

Smita touched his hand and said, 'yes, it was a moment of trial for us. For both of us, I thought, I was beyond redemption but . . . I didn't come to the worst.'

'Whom should I thank for your preservation?'

'They could do anything to me. Tear me into shreds.'

'Smita, please don't talk like this. I could stick to you despite that.'

'You don't have to tell me.' She beamed confidence, 'I feel like crying. But I wouldn't. It is not decent.' She constrained her tears. Her oval cheeks got only a faint strain of tears.

'Fight within and fight without', Smita remarked.

'I'm thinking of a big procession through the town. May be it draws the attention of people. Rajeev shifted from the personal to the impersonal.

People are passive spectators. Perhaps they have lost faith in agitations. They think it's all humbug. It's all good for nothing.

Rajeev seemed to be fighting with something irrelevant to his thought content.

'Yes, they think it's job of the politicians to manage all things. They show no concern with the affairs of the country. They don't go beyond the headings of newspapers.'

Smita was quite confident of what she spoke. She no longer gave the impression of being a mere college girl. She had her own ideas and line of thinking. Suddenly she gave a new direction to the conversation.

'And Ajeet is being helped by political rogues. I'm sure there are shadowy figures looming large and dim at the background.' Smita sounded more authentic because she had been through an ordeal.

Rajeev grew more contemplative and retrospective. His mind spanned over a period of four years in college.

'Yes, now I begin to undestand. You remember, Ajeet always misled students. He disuaded them from attending classes and appearing in examinations. Such students become popular. Such moves appeal to our students—escape from studies and hardwork. And now what do you propose to do?' Smita's face was now bereft of personal sentiments.

'I'll involve students in a big procession. Let them be involved in right and bigger issues. They can be channelized.' Tripathee and Rajeev came out of their snappy slumbers and joined the discussion. Final touches were imparted to the procession to be organized.

9

It was rather cloudy with scattered clouds racing over the sky. A soft, breeze intervened at intervals touching the cool fringes of the day. It was a phenomenon undergoing a constant change. Rajeev was touched. Perhaps his mind and heart did not move in the usual, mechanical way. Most of us operate our minds in one track manner without admitting a touch of creativity. It is the usual, the visible, the common place touch to the outer fringers of our brains. We hardly probe the dark reserviour of the sub-conscious containing possibilities of new wholes.

Gradually we grow blunted, opaque and in-sensitive towards finer shades of life. Rajeev was vibrant in his out look and so was Smita. They held the view that they could change the entire structure of the society. Rajeev, at the moment, was full of enthusiasm and was determined to give a new direction to the students of the college. Only if their energies are properly channelised. Only if? He must talk to them. He must persuade them. He must try to put a bit of idealism into them. He, at this juncture, thought of Gandhi. Whenever his spirits sagged he stretched his imagination to the lean human being.

He was an embodiment of eternal spirit in man craving for evolution. Gandhi didn't have any miracle about him. Neither did he wander in the world of abstractions. To him life was flesh and blood and his morality was an everyday affair, and not an isolated intellectual, inane excercise in words.

Rajeev spoke to fellow students, 'Dear friends, why not to join a peaceful march in the town? What's wrong? The town was already burnt and destroyed. You kept mum. Krishna was burnt to death. You didn't object.

'The march will be under a canopy of strict moral discipline. We can raise strikes against all sorts of unjust causes for our selfless achievements. We can be misled by seld-styled, selfish student leaders.'

His words had unmistakable impact. The students were moved.

Young minds are full of zest and goodness if they are given proper guidance. Students were swayed with words to a gradual crescendo.

It was four O'clock when faint shadows of the arriving evening manifested themselves. At this moment they barely strived for their existence. The text was full of life with the presence of two hundred students clad in simple items. They were instructed not to smoke or raise any untoward noise. Their faces must carry the impression of being devoted. They should not be trivial in any way. Triviality brings non-commitment and non-commitment leads to failure.

Rajeev's voice touched an emotinal pitch. The march was to touch the hardened hearts of indifferent citizens.

The marchers were spell-bound and Rajeev's voice was abruptly snapped by the movement of another pair of lips. The rough lips carried a lot of beard around them. The face was lost in thought and movement. Such faces, of course, are becoming rarer in our country. We have now faces in a hurry lost into exteriors of life. Perhaps those old moments of intro-spection are lost in speed. Life is being lived because it has to be lived. It is a sort of ritual of speed where all human commitments have become passive and irrelevant. Tripathee was a kind of philosopher, a youngman given to contemplation. His voice often wore in a monolithic seriousness. 'Draw your attention to rallies organised by our leaders. Political stunts. There are there either to establish popularity or achieve some selfish political end. They fail to move masses from within. It's just an exercise—a show business—a big crowd to be photographed in newspapers or put up on the small screen. They can go on a rampage aginst something valuable to your education.'

Tripathee talked to fellow students.

'Our march is moral, ethical and is to bring about a change. It is a fight against the powerful and the unjust.'

Idealism in youth has its complete sway and impact. It carries adolscent minds into a world of the most beautiful fabrications. Youth is impatient to build-up something new according to his dreams.

It was already five O'clock. Evening with its myriad shadows was about to descend like a shadowy figure. The students stood in two rows. Their faces bore expression of solemn aspects. It was to rack the sleeping conscience of the town. May be something happens? A beautiful march to draw the attention of people.

10

Smita and Rajeev were in the lead followed by Tripathee and Rajesh. They carried baners. They were soaked in an emotion of great sweep. The cause was solemn. A police van accompanied the marchers. It was preceeded by a jeep housing S.D.M. of the town. In case, something untoward happened, some little incident leading to violence. Then the marchers are to be restrained. The rout of the procession was already chalked out. Smita and Rajeev exchanged looks of tenderness and commitment. Emotional people have a lot of inner strength despite their obvious pitfalls. At times they bring themselves to the level of the earth. They find an equation with the earth but slowly they raise themselves and get engaged in their involvements. Rajeev was also made of the same metal. He vividly recollected the day of destruction when the town was left to wild tremours of human anarchy and anger. Perhaps the destructive, the irrational is more powerful in man, if once it lashes out. There is no end to its flaring up. Rajeev's mind wondered over the termination of vast civilizations. These had also fallen a prey to the irrational in man. Smita's face was taut with an emotion better felt by her. She mused over her position and concluded that she was no longer a girl of the four walls. The marchers were already on the half dilapedated roads of the town. There were occasional traffice jams as small crowds stood to witness the marchers. Some of them muttered in low-voiced grudenes, Processions are a source of nuisance and inconvenience. Students have no business to group themeselves like this.

Another by-stander clad in kurta supported the floating view. Teachers have lost their hold on students.

And how about parents? They have no say. Yes. we are fed-up with strikers. No studies, only strikes.

A thin voice came swimming across the crowd, The march is well-maintained. No slogans. No indiscipline. Peaceful march.

The march came to an abrupt standstill. The path was rendered narrower because of the repairs on the road.

Some rickshawallas spoke in hushed tones, Last year these students stoned rickshawallas. It was during a strike, their leadrs had attacked rickshawallas.

Noise and loot! Leaders went unpunished. My rickshaw was not repaired. Big loss. No body was responsible. I went to Thana. I was pushed away. Where is justice? The listener responed, we the poor, have to suffer a lot. We are always victims.

The rickshawala continued his complaint.

Rickshaw damaged, no money, no medicine for my wife.

He suddenly stopped talking and was impressed by the marchers in front of him. They seemed to be lost in something serious and greater. A steady movement of the evening had already taken a heavey toll of the sunlight. The burnt out ends of the hot day were cooling down sending respite to frayed nerves.

The march had already created a peaceful stir in the town. Shopkeepers stood by the roadside to have a full view of the procession and some of the onlookers tried. Locate their words in the march. Some shutters were closed down and then later on flying open as the fears of the shopkeepers were allayed. The walking policeman were in a mood of relaxation.

There was a sudden, sharp turn to the road. The turn was connected with two comparatively blind lanes. Their passages were narrow as if belonging to by gone days of the town. A ruffling noise rose in a subdued manner. Ten of them appeared like a lightening. Their faces safe under thick coverings didn't even give a glimpse of their identities. The attack on the marchers was sudden and operative. The ranks were defiled leaving many crying injuries. The uninformed protectors were unable to chase the invaders. Scattered voices rose like ripples. The pebbled road witnessed a drama of hurrying foot-steps and muffled voices. The attack was so quick and sudden that some of the present there were rendered emotionally opaque. A lot of bouncing of emotion sad thoughts. A few received head-injuries fit for immediate hospitalization. Smita rolled into dust at the extreme of the road. It resulted in a big jolt to the traffic allowing only a vehicle or two to sneak away.

Rajeev, some how or other, escaped only with minor injuries. Rajesh was still supple in his movents. He joined Rajeev in talking a quick toll of the attack. Some of them were to be romoved immediately. Some of the onlookers were pleaded and asked to cooperate. Most of them were evasive and rushed away at the mention of the slightest help.

Rajesh gave out a sudden yell, 'here, come, Rajeev. Look at Smita. The injury seems to be severe. She is almost unconscious. Put her on rickshaw. If no rickshaw man is ready, we must carry her on our shoulders? She can't stand more bleeding.'

Rajeev touched his fore-head to locate a faint ooze of blood-trickle. Smita was carried away to hospital. There was a sort of panic creeping into the hearts of people. A shadowy figure loomed large before them taking myriad shapes as if there were some one operating the strings of their destiny. Students on the road raised a hue and cry but didn't grow violent. Strange! There very students had raised strikers followed by stray incidents of minor violence. They had indulged in hooliganism and now?

Rajeev and Tripathee became over-acitve in handling the situation. Rajeev approached a group of rickshawallas, 'Why? Are you afraid? We are also like you. Why don't you transport the injured? No harm will come to you.'

They hesitated. Rajeev chided them affactionately, 'We are fighting for you. Our fight, is your fight.'

'No . . . no . . . A rickshaw man spoke in husky tones, Earlier we have been beaten by strikers. We had to pay *chanda* also.'

Tripathee was rather impatient, 'Don't worry. No trouble to you. You are arguing and the injured are dressed. No love for others? Don't you fear God?'

There was only a margin of response from them. They looked at one-another as to who should bell the cat. A rickshawalla came forward, hesitated and then took a leap towards the injured. Others followed him. The onlookers then lent support to them.

All around there were zig-zag patches of light and darkness. The road was blocked for the time being. There was hushed up silence in the distant corners of the road. The policemen had walked in the direction of the attackers. More policemen arrived there. The crowd must disappear, otherwise it could become an ugly situation. It might turn violent. But their fears were allayed. The students did not show any resentment. On the other hand, they tried to maintain their ranks in order to proceed further.

The S.D.M. jumped into the arena and shouted at them. 'You are not allowed to proceed further. You must disperse. Situation is tense. Your peace march is terminated. Go back. Deposit the injured for medical aid. We can't take any risk with your security.'

There was a sudden swell in the crowd. Parents of the students had made a dash towards the critical spot.

The S.D.M. was now in a fix. How to get rid of the crowd? He ordered firing in the blank. It worked. The spot looked deserted in half an hour.

11

The small room in the close vicinity of fields was given a decent look. Sooryakant was expected at any moment. Situation is to be reviewed and given a new direction. There must be discussions. Ajeet as usual was to play role of great importance because he was the closest to the leader. His council mattered, his voice created sensation and planning yielded results. A close-door meeting. All of them were alerted by the rise of small dust generated by the scudding of a vehicle. Unmistakably Sooryakant was there to keep up his appointment with them. He always comes alone. His activities are a sort of holy pact among them. The discussion takes place in his presence otehwise Ajeet and his followers never discuss anything. In fact Ajeet and his friends have no political leaning. They are hardly concerned with the turn of events in the country. They can hardly express anything on the current problems. They feel that they have an assignment yielding them bread, wine and a lot of money. Sooryakant must have brought these assests for them. Expectancy rose like the emerging tune of a song. Sooryakant came out of his car and shook hands with each one of them. Only Ajeet came forward to receive him. He was taken into the room and given the central chair. The master planner must be given the pivotal position otherwise the project will totter.

Ajeet narrated the attack on the marchers. 'I have already collected information from various sources. The S.D.M. himself came to me to talk about the happenings.

'Sir, he did a lot for us. Faithful. He allowed us to escape otherwise he could have ordered firing.' Ajeet spoke rather submissively.

'That was expected of him. He is my man. His future is connected with my planning.'

Sooryakant heaved a deep sign of boost and gave the impression of being triumphant.

'I have won great battles only like this. Battles are to be fought. One has to be practical these days. Those days are gone.'

'Which days, Sir?' Ajeet gave a minor chuckle to himself.

The leader fell into a mood of brief rumination. He was lost somewhere. His lower lip was moving and eyes were wondering over vast-fields.

'Yes, there were days when our brothers observed some sort of moral scruples. For us the struggle is naked.'

He was quiet for several minutes and then addressed, 'Ajeet, Rajeev is adamant. He was already been knocked down twice but he is adamant. We can't afford to ignore him. The town is already in turmoil. It's an atmosphere of doubt and suspicion.'

'Don't worry, sir. It's for us to set him right. We wouldn't allow his idealism to go a long way. He thinks Gandhi will take him for off.'

Ajeet's way of expression was of controlled wilderness. Yet he managed to laugh in a strange manner exposing his alliance with negative forces.

'Most of them are injured. They are in hospital. At least now they can't raise a procession. The Government might order an enquiry.' Ajeet looked at his mentor with a kind of raised expectancy.

'Don't worry about the so-called enquiry. After all the Chief-minister himself can't make all enquiries. He depends upon reports, we know. Let me not explain much.'

He put a restraint on his tongue and looked at them with confidence.

'No harm meant to you. Well done all of you. The march went to dogs. It's difficult to reorganise, Rajeev is worried about Smita. We should not have hurt her, at least.'

Ajeet couldn't help betraying a bit of sentiment.

'We could have spared her. She is the worst sufferer and now she is hospitalized.'

'Ajeet, you seem to be showing extra concern for her. Why? Is there anything special? May be during her kidnapping.'

'Please, Sir. Don't derive any special meaning. It's human.' The others sat listening. They were men of action and not of thought. Their main aim was to execute Ajeet's planning. That is what they were meant for. They had no interest in any kind of discussion, perhaps there was blockade to ideas offered by them. Yet they wouldn't betray. They wouldn't expose their underground activities. They left one after the other and Ajeet and Sooryakant were left to themselves.

'Ajeet, any soft corner for Smita.'

'No sir, in a way, yes?'

'Wish to win her over. She is made of some metal. The metal that sometimes bends but is never broken. But . . .'

'But what?'

'She is devoted to Rajeev. I know it. I feel attached. May be . . . may be . . . one day.

Every human is capable of sentiments. You are not an exception Ajeet.'

'Sir, let us drop this topic. It's personal . . . too personal. I have an idea.'

'What is that?' The leader beamed with an expectancy.

'Sir . . . you better visit the injured. Go to Smita. Say a few soft words. I always like that. I can't go. They know me thoroughly. I'll remain unconvincing.'

There was some pondering on the part of the big leader. And then suddenly he expressed his appreciation of the suggestion. 'I'll go. Of course. Why shouldn't I go? After all I have connections with the public. It's different that I'm not in the saddle but . . . I'm concerned. I'll take some gifts for them. That's the best way to win them over.' Sooryakant fluttered his eye-lids and tried to look straight into the situation. The situation was complex and tedius. The blame will go to the ruling party. They can't escape the stigma of violence. Why can't they control violence? This is the first question that swims before a common man. He does not go beyond the apparent. He bases his conclusions on the obvious or reporting done in newspapers.

Reports about the march have appeared in various newspapers. A peaceful march marred by anti-social elements. Sooryakant must prove that he is one of the defeated candidates and without him the constituency is not peaceful. Such ideas raced in his mind.

Ajeet spoke, 'Sir, your presence is felt. People over there feel that there is someone. Someone whom we can't ignore.'

He was pleased. Some people must make their presence vital, whatever might be the means.

'Ajeet, your work is excellent. You'll be amply rewarded. Here is some money. Distribute it among your friends. Enjoy your life, we must win.'

He strode out of the room followed by Ajeet. He was not in his customary mood. His mind was lost somewhere between his actions and lectures he had been delivering.

The driver opened the door of the car to allow him sit on the back-seat. Ajeet gave him a folded hand send off without uttering anything. The vehicle found its way through the *kuchcha* road. He reached his bunglow and found four of his partymen seated in the porch.

12

On his arrival in the porch of his bunglow, his partymen stood up leaving their cups of tea on the table.

'Soorya ji, where did you go? I suppose . . .' said one of them in a rather pleasing manner.

'I'm sorry. I went out just like that. To have a car ride in the open. You park the car somewhere near fields and then have a stroll. A stroll to solve political problems of the country.' The other partyman did not lag behind in starting that with the leader.

'By the way . . . what about events in the town?'

'Such situations are normal in a developing country and democracy. Personally I'm dead against voilence. People have a right to express themselves.'

Their conversation took the shape of a mini-group discussion.

'Rajeev has support neither of a political party nor of a political person of stature.'

'He is doomed. Without political support, agitations in India don't mean anything.'

'That's true. Who bothers about the sentiments of common people? And what about Rajeev?'

'Just a slip of a boy! And Smita?'

'I tell you. I learn she has two more sisters. No family worthy of mention will welcome them.'

'By the way, What's Smita's fault? Has she done anything immoral? To sit with three boys in the tent for nights together. And then to be kidnapped. Who knows what has been done to her? Even the most educated, modern, open-minded of us have this line of thinking. The attitude is inherent in us. We fling back to the same obsessions. What do you think Sooryakant Ji? You are one of the enlightened ones.'

'Such discussions add a flavour only on the drink—table. Fix it up to-night.'

Sooryakant gave a ready approval with a massive nodding of his head. A wave of jubilation swept over their faces.

'By the way, how about visiting the injured?'

'A great idea . . . Sooryakant Ji. After that we can have drinks.'

'Excellent . . . Two of you to the bazar'

'Buy some gifts, fruits and sweets.'

'O.K. here is some money.'

They got ready for a visit to the victims of the peaceful march.

Sooryakant did his best to spread one of the softest smiles on his face. He must be extra-nice to the victims of the march. He must visit Smita. She is the worst victim of all.

The group visited other victims also and distri-buted gifts to them. The next day newspaper carried the minor news in a minor way. The group came back to their starting point and drinks were fixed up according to the plans.

Sooryakant was in a mood of contemplation. He was the architect of their injuries. What for? He could be secretive or would disclose his mind not to more than two or three persons. He believed in the old adage—everything is fair in love and war.

Drinks were fixed up in the big lawn. They sat cosy and comfortable in reclining chairs. No one uttered anything in the first hour. They were lost in their respective dreams of consciousness. Drinks sometimes push us into inner recesses of mind and make us eloquent from within.

Sooryakant had decided to be the least participant in the talks to follow. It was something usual with him and his political supporters.

One of them came out with definite views, 'The students have been served right. They had no business to deal with political issues. Look at their mis-calculations. An agitation without any political support! Nothing but humbug and foolish.' One of them muttered the words in a very candid and coherent manner. His lips were steady during the flow of words, 'Sooryakant Ji, You have won the hearts of the students. They will definitely be voting for you in the next elections. You really know how to deal with voters, Really!'

Their faces were flushed and minds agitated. There was no count of glasses of whisky that were being poured through their throats. Sooryakant is quite liberal with them as far as consumption of liquor was concerned. He knows that politics these days can not he run on the basis of principles. Suddenly he thought of Rajeev, a slip of a boy, out to confront the entire corrupt system.

Sooryakant's friends were quite vigilant about his moods and the rise and fall of his thoughts going on in his mind. One of them grew quite violent in thinking and his expression, A boy like Rajeev is still alive? He has no political backing. He should have been finished by now. We are political leaders. We have seen all political ups and downs. Still Rajeev is surviving.

The speaker of this quote lost his balance of mind and words almost drowned in the perfumes rising in his stomach reaching his brain. He seemed to be in a state of uncertain mood giving expression to his blackest thoughts.

'If you wish, Sir, . . . I can get Rajeev murdered. A very petty job!'

Sooryakant lit a cigrette and kept on looking at the burning match-stick and then spoke with a shake of his head, 'No . . . no . . . I don't wish him to be murdered. He is already finished. His agitation gone to dogs! ah! ah! He wants to revive Gandhi. He mentions Gandhi to followers.'

'I mean students. They are not mature . . . mere bookish knowledge is different from the one we practise.'

'I don't think you should bother that much for that boy. Not worth your thought . . .'

Another of his followers flattered him. 'His tent is already up-rooted. I say . . . what a useless agitation? I say . . . what's the use of such agitations?'

'It's not your fault, Sir. It's the fault of the stuff gone in your tummy. Mischief maker!' Aren't you drinking with us?

'And that Smita . . . Sali . . . Why did you spare her? She should have been raped. I can do this job for you. I will leave her finished for ever.'

'I say . . . What is her existence? Two sisters, father and a mother. They can't run their family. These girls will become prostitutes . . . otherwise how can they eat their food?'

The servant walked in with a fresh supply of liquor.

At least they were cautious not to express their precious views in the presence of servants.

The night was partially visible in the lawn because of the various dim sources of light. They viewed one-another through intoxicated vibrations of mind. A sort of atmosphere in the lawn conducive to violent and nefarious thinking.

One is tampted to go back to those days of sanctity and sacrifice when Gandhi led movements. There must have been some impelling spirit moving the hearts of people. How did they make supreme sacrifices? Yes . . . why did they? The entire country was elecrified with a moving spirit, a wave lifting masses on the plane of self sacrifice and love for the country. Not a single idea of this kind passed through Sooryakant's mind. He must keep the reins of the town in his hands by hook or crook. He must put different groups under his thumb. His thoughts did not travel beyond these premesis. Nefarious elements of the town seek shelter under him. Where is the distinction between good and bad? Between moral and immoral? All considerations have gone to dogs. Yes. thrown away like the riff-raff, like the rotten stiff of on practical utility.

At the moment they are poised upon a pivot—destroy Smita and her family. Why? They are not supposed to raise their voice. They must compromise with Krishna's death. They must forget him for ever.

In the morning they landed softly, peacefully before General Hospital of the city and went straight to one of the wards. The injured were already admitted to different wards of the Hospital. There was Smita with her bandaged head. Her eyes were open and were looking into a sort of vacancy.

Sooryakant's arrival was announced quietly and he walked in peacefully without much noise. One of his followers carried packets.

'And you Smita . . . Beti. Hurt much? It's rather sad. Violence in democracy is to be finished. Beti, can you recognise the culprits? I'll see them punished.'

Smita just lay on the pillow without any utterance of significance. Perhaps her physical condition did not allow her to answer the queries. With a nod she denied the existence of culprits to her knowledge.

'And Rajeev Ji. I must congratulate you for undertalking such a bold step. Criminals must be exposed to the public view.'

Rajeev just looked at the speaker honestly. His face did not tell any story. It was poised and normal.

'Why don't you help us, Sir?'

Later on, Rajeev was repentant at his own words. Political help was beyond the perview of his agitation. One of the packets was put on the bed where Smita lay brooding. She was given a ceremonial blessings by Sooryakant. His parting words ran like this. 'If you help me in the next elections, I'll not allow such situations. I'll put an end to violence and criminals will be discarded politically. Only if Rajeev ji gives me support. I promise to carry your ideals to masses. I promise.'

Rajeev accompanied him to the door and gave a send off.

Sooryakant's followers spoke in unison.

'Sooryakant Ji, we don't mind doing anything for you. We are your true servants. Our main aim is to keep you in saddle. Once you are in power, money pours in. Women, wine follow. What else do we want? We don't mind the means to achieve our ends.'

Their tongues stammered and clattered. Their minds roamed or sank according to intoxicating waves in their minds. No logic, no philosophy, no moral perception and vision. Only strong lust to be near the chair, to keep Sooryakant happy. Everything else was to be used, discarded according to the situations.

13

It was two O'clock in the receeding phase of the night. The stars were brighter on the far-off corners of the globe. They seemed to make their presence more eloquent on the quieter phase of the night. Rajeev was awake and restless. He stood watching the movement of heavenly bodies and seemed to co-relate them with fortunes of earthly beings. Was there any connection?

Are we governed from the above? Why do drastic changes take place? Perhaps it was all beyond his common understanding. A cool breeze lifted him above his philosophical broodings. Smita was on her way to recovery and many of the injured were yet to get off their beds. There were news in most of the dailies but no editorials. A probe into the incident was likely to be ordered. There was a lot of dismay and depression in the town. They felt suppressed before an unknown Dragon ready to eat them up. Rajeev was lost in a maze of conjectures. Who could be responsible for all the mishaps meted out to him? And why should he go against them? Yes, Ajeet full of mischief and misconduct. But he could not trigger off violence and mishaphs on such massive scales. Should we abandon resistance?

The town was cowed down. None to offer resistance. The officials were more concerned with their office routine. Moreover they were not supposed to offer resistance as public figures or crusaders. Their primary job was to keep the town in trim.

A strange mental anguish filted Rajeev's mind. Was he there to set everything right? Time was out of joint. Suddenly he thought of Hamlet's predicament and his ultimate destruction. Was he to go the same way? And what about Smita? She was already out of the four walls of the house and poised for a public venture. Despite a series of pit-falls she had encountered, she had not dismayed. Rajeev's emotional fervour was pitched to a sensitive strong. Should he withdraw and settle down to a life of routine commonalities? If Gandhi had thought like this, the country would not have seen the dawn of emancipation. It was none of his jobs. Then whose job? He tried to understand the historical process. Curiously enough most of us remain passive spectators. He was watchful and observant about his thinking. There piled up a lot of tension in his mind and he didn't know how to get out of it. He didn't know how to arrange his ideas as they came with a lot of on-rush of feelings without any check.

People need a guide to lead them. Does he have all those qualities to become a leader? Already there were rumours in the town.

He and Smita were being projected as the future successful candidates for elections. They must fight elections. About Smita there was a lot of back-chat.

The girl has already spoiled her family. She is a curse to her parents. She should have kept herself under the bounds of family ties. She should not have bothered her aging parents. Poor creatures! Rajeev has already spoiled her. Now she is not fit for marriage. We can't trust boys and girls these days. Old ladies of the Mohalla weren't scarred of commenting at all.

'This family of Smita's should be thrown out of the Mohalla, Slut three of them. How do they earn their bread?'

One-eyed old man of the street often came out with his nefarious thoughts. He tried to create an atmosphere against this family. May be he had some grudge against them? But he was sometimes contradicted by saner elements. 'It is none of our business. Why can't Smita join politics? They are not taking anything from us. Moreover girls should be encouraged to battle their life.' All sorts of opinions floated in the Mohalla and the town. No one in the Mohalla thought that Krishna had been a riot-victim. The family needed support. Only Rajeev had come to their real help but he weaned away Smita to politics.

14

It was six O'clock in the evening when the sky began to look grey and dark. The corners of the sky were rather blank without the presence of dust. Rajeev was walking through lanes towards Smita's house. The house was rather isolated, if not physically but morally and socially. There was something unusual about house because of Smita's active participation in politics. She had taken a recourse to something which most of the girls were not supposed to. Moreover she had violated the moral precinets of the town. Rajeev was reluctant to walk in not because of any moral considerations but Smita's sisters and parents. They must have cursed him profously. He was the architect of their misfortunes. He walked through an unswept lane leading to a narrow *Kachcha* pavement terminating at the threshold of Smita's house.

There she was in the same room cosy on her bed. Her forehead had a plastic bandage and there was passive cheerfulness on her face. She gave a curious look to Rajeev and nodded him to sit down. There ensued serveral moments between them. Perhaps they were in the grip of a seething turmoil.

Smita suddenly became tender towards him, 'You shuldn't expect much from my people. They certainly dislike you. They have no understanding of your ideals and aspirations. Better don't argue with them. Otherwise, I'm with you, Rajeev.' There were tears in her eyes. She touched his hand tenderly and spoke.

'Rajeev, when woman surrunders, she is ready for anything. Perhaps there was something smouldering in me, you gave a direciton in a channel.'

Meanwhile the two sisters rushed in bearing stern expressions on their faces. Rekha pounced upon him. 'Are you our friend or enemy? Why do you come here? Are you to finish our home? Smita had a narrow escape from death. In the hospital, I contained myself but now there is no check.'

She was extremely defiant in her attitude towards him. Misery sometimes makes us extremely angry with ourselves. We are not able to reckon with the mysterious manifestations of the sub-conscious through myriad ways unknown to us. Smita looked at Rajeev with a lot of understanding and kept her expressive in his face. He was rather feeling down-cast because of the constant shower of curses at him. He dared not face Smita's parents. Rekha continued in the same vein, 'For God's sake spare us. Leave us alone. Let's face starvation and death. Father's already coughing beyond sleep, we don't know.'

Rajeev went in a great mental anguish and he did not know what to do. Moreover he didn't want to extract money through foul means. But he could not evade his responsibility to this family. He was in a way responsible for dragging Smita into the present crisis.

Rekha and Sona were still in fumes and frets. They were perhaps out to extract an oath atleast from Smita regarding her future participation in politics.

Sona came forward and spoke in aggressive tone. 'You better don't visit us. We have already earned a bad name in the town. We are stared at, commented upon and ridiculed.'

There was a pin-drop silence in the small attic and a lot of mental turmoil in them.

Rajeev was down in spirits and full of dismay. He didn't know how to set things right. Smita, so far, didn't know how to shape her impulses. The moment was gaining tension for her. How to resolve the crisis?

Rajeev was relentless. He didn't know how to proceed further in his way of thinking. Evil lay asbright as the day light and even then he couln't do anything. Should he fall flat on his kness and accept everything like this? He could live a life of no protests, and no thinking. He could just live like lots of people without thinking. He could become a part of the rat-race and live a life of abject surrender. He suddenly got up and looked at Smita. There was the same depth of feeling and understanding that she always encountered in her eyes.

'Why don't you sit down Rajeev?'

The two sisters were shocked to hear Smita.

'I don't know what to do? I'm lost Smita. I don't know how to fight further . . . what to do? I don't know . . . What do do? I'm surrounded by evil. They are too strong for me. Yes, too strong. I feel like a haunted, trapped, animal.'

The End

'The Migrant' is episodic in content and outlook. Though it gives the impression of being semi-autobiographical, yet it is purely a creative work born out of imagination. Names of characters in the novel are purely fictitious. It sets out to offer glimmering landscapes of Austrailian and Indian cultures. It is interesting and full of movement.

Dedicated to

Rev. Martin. Irene

Ashok Sharma

Special Thanks

Ashu and Shalini Nagpal

THE MIGRANT

Prof. Dharam Pal

1

He observed a few patches of clouds in the sky. They seemed to be strangers to one another and directionless because they cannot locate exact spots and faces. They are ignorant of the exact lanes leading to open voids.

Patches of clouds over the vast expanses of the sky and below the unfathomed deep sea taking different hues. He sighed to himself and was suddenly reminded of shelly's poetic utterance:—'of what scene are we spectators and actors?'

He inhaled a deep puff of the smouldering cigarette held in between his fingers and cast a lonely glance around. He became sensitively aware of the vast loneliness in man's heart; loneliness of grief and loneliness of birth and death. Loneliness of death gave him a fear of high intensity.

A young waitress swam into his ken. He looked at her youthful figure and grew a bit contemplative.

'Do you need anything else?' The young waitress blinked her eyes in half smile.

He spoke rather loudly—'When old age shall this generation waste thou shall remain amongst other woe.'

The waitress was rather amazed and confused at the utterance. She took half a step forward. He looked at her keenly and spoke that we grow old in age but remain young in a painting, if painted by a painter.

The waitress did not betray any sensitivity for the lines spoken by him.

Yes, he was seated in the premises of the Art-Gallery without any acquaintance.

The road below was alive with a constant flow of humanity. He silently observed that flow on the road. To flow is life. It may be a flow in the ocean or flow on the road escorted by sky scrapers. A curious combination of creativity. Nature is master-mind to which there is no end. To some extent human brain follows the footsteps of nature.

He felt a strong urge to talk to someone but there was no one known to him. A stranger talking to another stranger does not make a comfortable human situation. Suddenly he was reminded of the painted canvass of Beatrice and Dante in room number 3 of the gallery. A powerful, intimate impulsive sensation stormed his sub-conscious.

Beatrice, a beautiful woman, stepping out of the threshold of the house. A strange bewilderment reflected in her eyes directed at Dante. The two stand on the verge of permanent separation. The creator and the created drifting in opposite directions. He felt an overwhelming desire to share his poetic feelings but there was none to listen to his communications. He must talk.

'Any one occupying this chair . . .' A question echoed in his ears. He looked up to a see a beautiful dame talking to him.

'Oh! No'. He wanted to talk to her but she had already given a push to the chair. In his own country, he can converse even with strangers. Moreover he has many old friends with whom he has spent many moments of joys and sorrows.

He deserted his chair in a jiffy and made way to the toilet and then to another level in the Art-Gallery. He rushed towards an escalator in the downward direction. There was a conglomeration of boys, girls, men and women.

He experienced an inner throb at the sight of the conglomeration. They were lost in the web of chatting and sipping coffee.

He made up to a middleaged lady—'what's on? Why is this gathering?'

She enthused her tongue—

'Oh, you are not aware, a seminar on world religions about their birth, growth, influence and decay, A long and interesting history. A strange narration, well-quoted and supported with evidence.'

Her face was lit with a half formed smile.

Meanwhile another lady stepped into the arena of the conversation.

'Oh! you too can join, prepare some coffee for yourself. What is your name?'

'Avadhesha.'

'Hinduism is also a part of discussion. Go, go for coffee and then enter the auditorium.'

Avadhesha was extremely happy at this co-incidence. The author, Deepak Chopra's statement swam into his head—'co-incidences matter much.'

He flew in the direction of the coffee-table. He thought of his own country where religious congregations are followed by lot of prayers and others rituals.

'How long will it go?'

He was back with his cup of coffee and snacks.

'Three weeks, every Saturday. Not a free event.'

'Price of the event is 100 dollars.'

Avadhesha was feeling bewildered and frozen at the price of the event. He felt amazed at the curiosity of the audience who were spending 100 dollars for the price of the event.

He sipped coffee rather hurriedly and entered the big lecture-room.

He could locate a seat in the vicinity of a middle aged lady and made himself quite comfortable there. The lady appeared to be of benign temperament as she registered a faint smile on her face.

The lecture-room was vastly filled with multicultural audience. Right on the front stood the speaker near the dias. His voice was audible and there stood a huge screen for illuminating communications.

Avadhesha was thrilled to see Buddha in a state of trance. People wrongly think that Christnity is intolerant of other religions and cultures. Buddha's contribution toward man's salvation is immensely significant.

The speaker in the hall was eloquent, illustrative and expressive. He was explicit on the influences of other religions that have impacted humanity at large.

He elaborated conflicts of religions that flare up from time to time been inflicting and damaging mankind alike. The speaker's utterances were a curious mixture of humour and seriousness. At times a pronounced laughter or faint smiles or loud giggles responded to the speaker's remarks.

But invariably he was in a serious strain in his historical perspectives of the growth of world religions. The screen on the stage was lit with pictures and images. The speaker talked for forty five minutes and kept the audience captivated and attentive.

As the speaker gave last touches to his discourse the audience began to ooze out of the auditorium.

The audience became wide open when it entered the lobby. Avadhesha was feeling highly over-joyed at the most unexpected opportunity of mixing with a good crowd. It was a kind of psychological relief to him.

He looked around and was dazed to look at the counter. Two young beautiful girls were serving liquor to the audience.

Avadhesha hung his head, fluttered his eyes-lids in vast amazement at this sight. In his own country religious discourses are given finishing touches with 'Prasad'. At the most, the audiences in India are offered pure vegetarian food called 'Bhandara'.

He glanced at ladies and gentlemen standing in small group drinking and chatting. Avadhesha's glance caught a lady. She was fair and bobbed hair.

She was of a mediocre height and well dressed. She bore a friendly expression on her face and seemed to be well-disposed even towards strangers.

Avadhesha turned around to see the lady confronting him with a bewitching smile.

She spoke to him.

'Feeling lonely? Completely lost? Not in a happy situation?'

She drew towards Avadhesha and addressed him.

'Don't feel perplexed. Don't feel lonely. I am with you.'

Avadhesha was wonder-struck at the spontaneous advances of the lady.

'Which country?'

'From India.'

'But you don't look like Indian.'

'My son and daughter live here.'

'That's fine.'

'What job in India?'

'Teaching in a college.'

'That's fine.'

She suddenly implanted a kiss on his cheek. His red-wine glass registered a minor shaking.

Avadhesha again looked at the lady. Her complexion was fair and attractive. Her eyes carried an expression of eloquence and she glanced in quick succession.

She diverted Avadhesha's attention towards a middle-aged man. 'You go to Micheil.'

As Avadhesha went near him, he found his face was rugged. His nose and eyes suggested scholarly leanings. He was busy sipping drops of liquor. His eyes were a bit intoxicated but his face was without any impression of elevation.

Avadhesha accosted him with an intimate hand shake.

'You are from India. An eminent Indian writer is dead. I am missing his name.'

'Yes, the news was on the internet. But I can't recall the name.'

'Ruskin Bond?'

'Oh no . . . . He is not Indian. He lives in India.'

Avadhesha made many attempts to prompt Micheil's memory but failed.

'It's alright . . . ,' Avadhesha tried to divert Micheil's attention.

'You too write?'

'Yes, fiction.'

'O! that's fine.'

'My books are in the state Library of Sydney.'

'That's fine, Encouraging.'

By that time the lady had walked towards them.

She was equipped with a scrap of paper and pressed Avadhesha to scribble the titles of his books in the Library.

Avadhesha replied in a husky voice—'My books are in Hindi.

'In Hindi!'

An unknown voice buzzed his ears.

'Write down the titles of your books.'

'Languages do not matter. Literature is the common property of the mankind.'

And the lady implanted her lips several times on the other cheek of Avadhesha. The touch was soft and intimate.

He flushed but felt a sensation of inward joy. He felt rather exalted to be kissed by a lady in the crowd.

It was a unique experience for him because he had never come across such a situation in his life.

The web of human beings around them hardly looked at them.

Slowly the crowd was thinning down.

Avadhesha was to be in the creative company of the portraits of the Art-Gallery. He must look at portraits as he derives creative satisfaction from them.

He always felt a joy of its own kind in the company of mute eloquent artistic creations.

He entered an adjoining room. There he stood facing the portrait of a still house at the threshold of crossing lanes. The portrait was eloquent in its silence.

Avadhesha gave a stretch to his imagination and thought of time flown into oblivion. Suddenly his sub-conscious suggested T.S Eliot's poetic lines.

'Where is the life? We have lost in living?'

The portrait of a vast structure and the by-lanes stood evidence to time gone forever. 'Time is evil'—a sentence from Huxley's Ape and Essence swam into his sub conscious.

His mind captured the woman who had kissed his cheeks.

'What a surprise?'

He located the same lady coming towards him.

He beamed a smile at her with a lot of response.

'I am sorry, forgot to ask your name and other where-abouts. I am Irene. I work as guide in the Art-Gallery. My job is sponsored.'

'That's wonderful. I mean the place you work at is an ideal and beautiful place. Do you get any compensation of the sort?'

'Nothing, An inner satisfaction.'

Irene's face seemed to be in the grip of extreme joy. It was the manifestation of something different in her away from the mundane.

'Your name please?'

'Avadhesha—an Indian name.'

'O-Avadhesha'

'No, no—Avadhesha.

Names from different countries are difficult to pronounce.

'Never mind,' Avadhesha Spoke in low tones.

'Do you visit gallery quite often?'

Avadhesha gave a nodding assent.

He grew expressive in emotion, 'I relive aesthetic moments in the company of these portraits. Time is fleeting. Nothing to prevent its flight. It's dragging towards a void. It's the greatest irony of life on this planet. No one can fight the onslaughts of Time. Man has invented different systems of religions to confront the fact of death.

'I am reminded of a sentence from the novel—Dr. Zivago. Entire civilization has been created to confront one fact and that is the fact of death.'

Irene was impressed with what Avadhesha blurted out.

'O! you are quite philosophical. Your probing compels me to think but at the moment I am quite occupied. Time to lead a group to modern paintings.'

She spoke rather in flurried tones.

'I don't mind.'

'Please attend to your job.'

'See you later on.'

'See you.'

Avadhesha was much elevated at this chance—encounter with the lady.

It may lead to the binding of relationship.

A good emotional boost.

Avadhesha espied a group of men and women looking for Irene. The group consisted of men, women and children from different countries.

He was rather amazed to find so many people interested in paintings. Their eagerness to listen to Irene was commendable. On her arrival she was greeted by half expressed salutations.

Her sweet melodious voice captured the attention of the group. Her dim sweet voice vibrated in the hall.

'I propose to take you to the world of paintings. This small excursion will give an experience and a healthy escape from the day-to-day world. You will have glimpses of ancient as well as modern art.'

Each one of them was under the melodious impact of Irene's voice.

Impulsively Avadhesha too decided to be part of the group. He resolved not to face Irene's straight glances. He saw the Gallery blooming with people of different cultures.

In his own country Art-Galleries are never crowded. People prefer to go on pilgrimages to atone for their sins. All try to secure a safe birth in their next life.

The group headed by Irene entered the sections of ancient art. Irene looked at her best as if lit by an aesthetic glow. Avadhesha was rather sneaking after the group.

Irene alerted the group—'ladies and gentlemen! look at Buddha's statue in a state of trance. It looks divine and beautiful. It is the beauty of his soul that radiates spiritual glow towards us. But it is curious to know that his movements have inspired quite a number of creative artists to give them expression in different mediums.

'Look over there Buddha in a state of trance. First let me know if you are acquainted with Lord Buddha?'

A voice became audible. 'Yes, he is a great monk of India. He is known almost all over the world.'

Another man from the group spoke in a husky voice.

'Why, there is a Buddhist temple in Sydney. The worship is conducted in mandarin.'

'That's fine'

'I can talk about Buddha. There he sits in a sculptured form in a state of trance. Look at the divine peace on his face. It transcends pangs of birth, sufferings and event of death. It springs out of an intense meditation and concentration.

He was born in 'Kapilvastu.'A voice echoed from the group. Irene immediately responded, 'Welcome'.

A woman from the group uttered something in low tones, 'but he should not have left his beautiful wife Yashodra and Rahul his son. I belong to the land of Kamasutra'

The woman replied rather peevishly.

Avadhesha felt amazed at the lady's unwanted remark but fortunately the remark went almost above the heads of the small group of humanity.

Irene again took the lead, 'Look there ladies and gentlemen!'

'Buddha in a state of trance is an apostle of transcendental meditation. The painting indicates how Buddha achieved *Nirvana*.

'The absolute truth dawned upon him in moments of enlightenment. The moment was intense and culmination of all his broodings about the purpose of human life.

'Yes, there is a divine glow on his face.'

One among the audience responded to Irene's utterances about Buddha. After this, the group was led to another section of the Gallery. Avadhesha thought it would be better for him to retract from the scene.

2

A day of drizzling, when nature picked up different hues of her manifestations. None of us can prevent her taking different hues. Her power is expressed in many moods and spread outs that can be predicted but not prevented.

Homos sapiences watch and adjust and then forget also. But intrinsically nature remains potent and dynamic.

A sequestered park in the midst of constant flow of Sydney. A wooden shed dimly makes its existence visible if looked at intently.

There is a dim haze enveloping the prominent contours of the city. An old, shabby human being is seated under the shed. His face has lost his prominent features and the left out are a hotch-potch of intersecting lines. His eye-lids are like shutters beaten by stormy winds.

At time he mumbles to himself, 'I want to go back to India.'

'Yes India, My wife no longer breathing. My brother, sister, friends all in India. Here I am left alone. No one to share my feelings, sorrows. Loneliness is just like storm sweeping away my life.'

No listener was there.

Tears welled up in his eyes like a vast desert.

He gave a bit of movement to his limbs and dragged himself out of his sorrows. To his surprise, he located two birds in the vicinity of a bench.

He said to himself, 'I have witnesses to my sorrow.'

That imparted to him a kind of joy born out of spontaneous feelings.

'How long could I linger under the shed?'

They must be arriving home—his son and daughter-in-law.

He felt a tremor in his body and mind.

'How do they look at him?'

The very expression in their eyes sends him back to a hellish state of mind.

The words of his daughter-in-law operate like a crescendo of regret and negation to his feelings. She often gives a sinister twist to her lips and draws her words—'My dear aging father-in-law, Why do you nourish your craving for India? Your house premises is locked. By now it must be out of tune with its surroundings. Aren't you afraid of the lonely look of the deserted house?'

'But my friends . . .' the old man stammered. 'And there are big religious congregations giving a kind of mental solace.'

All this has become a part of his mental stock and imagination.

'Papa, your imagination is nothing but a paltry structure.

The world is changing very fast. It is not only in Sydney. It is true in India also.'

The old man had started talking to himself—'I must reach home as soon as possible. I must reach in time otherwise my son and his wife loose their tempers.'

Fortunately the drizzle had come to an end.

'I have tried my best to befriend people here. But no response, just winking of eye-lids and faint smiles. In this city all relationships are situational.'

A car on the road creased to a sudden halt. The old man's absent-mindedness was the author of this nasty situation. The driver of the car mumbled and gave a casual glance to the old man's fast balding head. And then he stepped away. The old man resumed his conversation with himself.

'Why can't I go back to India? I want to talk. I want to express myself. Everything, my loneliness, my sleepless nights. In my country people come to parks, chat a lot, share joys and sorrows.'

He hears his daughter-in-law talking—'Papa, do not talk of by gone days. Be a realist. Here we are with you, nothing to fear.'

Mr. Vinayak had walked several yards of foot-paths. The roads were drenched. Suddenly he came across a beautiful girl in her shorts.

He partly averted his looks and then fixed his gaze at the half naked-legs of the girl. He felt a momentary relief from the tension preying his nerves.

There was another shower pouring itself in all the nooks and corners of the area.

Mr. Vinayak hurriedly crossed the road and sheltered himself under a small shed. Just behind the shed stood a row of lonely houses inhabited by human beings. There prevailed a kind of silence least indicative of any human presence.

He gave a strong jerk to his dress to wipe away rain drops. He thought of his town in India where he was educated and lived. A streak of gleam flashed up on his face but he was actually aware of the conglomeration of zigzag lines on his forehead indicative of ravages of time.

Suddenly a feminine face stared at him and spoke to him. He at once recognized the face of his dead wife—Savita. 'Aren't you left all alone? That was exactly my apprehension about you, Intuitions sometimes become realities. Fears become moving features of life. But don't worry. You too are nearing the last episode of your life. We will be reunited.'

It was an eerie experience. His dead wife did speak to him.

A consolation! She dinned her words into his ears. For a few moments he was drowned in the vibrant area craved by his sub-conscious. It was consoling indeed.

A strong wind rose from the precincts of the sky. At times matter and mind sway in harmony. He must hurry up to escape his daughter-in-law's invectives. His son Rohan hardly checks his wife from expressing her anger with him.

Yes, he must visit a psychiatrist, He spoke to himself dimly. But he is left with no money through he is a pensioner. His money is brutally squeezed by his son and his wife.

She scolds him quite often, 'What for do you need money? We give you food and shelter. You wear proper cloths. We get your pension. Why don't you pray to God? You stand on the last edge of your life.'

'True, true but I need some money. Pocket expenses.'

'I know for what you need money. Sydney is filled with all types of temptations.'

He would feel highly mentally ignited but his inward wrath was of no consequence.

'To whom should I express my grief?'

He questioned himself time and again. Antone chekov's story 'Grief' often flashed in his mind. The son of a cab-driver was dead.

He was driven almost mad with grief. No one to share his deep anguish. He walked down to his horse to narrate the entire episode of his son's death. Once or twice he had tried to establish his relationship with his neighbors but his efforts came to a void. Most of his neighbors' are without elderly members. Only one Greek old man lives in his neighborhood. Whenever he talks to him language becomes a barrier between the two.

They do not find it convenient to communicate with each other. It is lost in the muddle of languages. One day the Greek bluntly told him, 'I can't converse with you. About you I can't talk to your son and daughter-in-law. They might give me a big jolt by telling me not to talk about the family.'

He was alerted about the ugly situation that might arise in his family.

Mild clouds in the sky darkened the evening earlier than the usual time. There were a number of bubbles on the pavement. They looked like toddlers peeping out of the mother's apron. Mr. Vinayak looked at them as if they held some consolation for him. His steps were steady at the prospect of meeting Rohan and his wife Kamla.

They must bewildered at his absence in this rough weather. As soon as he came across them, there was a shower of bitter words. Rohan was beyond his self control and almost pounced upon his father 'Is this the weather to be out? You are almost crazy. You have forgotten all norms of life. I wish you to go back to India. But there is none to take care of you.'

'I'll live alone.'

'O God! Give some sense to my father. He knows not what he says. His mind is not less than a rotten dustbin. Suppose he expires all alone in his Indian abode. The blame will be thrown at me. All my relatives including my dead mother are going to curse me.'

Mr. Vinayak deemed it better not to entangle himself in arguments with his own son.

He was afraid

Lest he should be seen, he stepped into the house and sat like a statue without betraying any emotion or reaction. His lips were tremulous without making any hearing audible.

Rohan flashed an intense look at him, 'Father, anything wrong? You want to say something?'

His tone was harsh and unintimate. The old man spoke in his creaky voice, 'I want to consult a psychiatrist.'

'Are you mad?'

'What for? I pass many sleepless nights and visualize nightmares.'

'This is your faulty fancy. You better pray to God.'

'I keep on praying to God. It doesn't help. I always feel that I am suffering from some mental aberration.'

'Nothing of the sort. Believe me, nothing of the sort.'

Vinayak's daughter-in-law suddenly interposed in the chain of dialogue.

'Daddy . . .' she made a frown sit upon her lips,' Do you know the fee of a psychiatrist? He is likely to recommend some test. It is definitely to increase the medical expense.'

Without the drizzle came to a stand still creating a sort of void, Vinayak sat like a culprit caught in the web of loneliness. He had the feeling of a culprit caught in the sinister net-work of circumstances.

'How does all happen?' He questioned the ways of destiny that man encounters. His philosophic musings took diverse directions. 'Are there stars governing man's ways? Who is the controller? Everyman's fate is cast in different way? God! you are mysterious and enigmatic. None can understand your ways.'

In a wave of excitement and boosted ego Vinayak uttered, 'What about my pension?'

Rohan's wrath was ignited at the mention of the word pension—'So you are boasting of that? What do you think is the cost of living in Sydney? It is quite expensive, everything costs money. Daddy—you should pray to God.'

'I do, but that's not enough. It doesn't give solace to my mind. I feel bewildered and restless. I need sharing of my feeling and thoughts. My mind craves for something and that keeps me depressed and sorrowful.'

The trio fell into an unusual quiet. The old man understood the main root of his predicament. Rohan and his wife were greedy about his pension. They clung to it like some wild animal preying on an innocent victim.

In India there are massive religious congregations. These may not be highly scientific but give some kind of consolation to people. Some kind of sense of belonging and sharing and that serves as a source of consolation.

Vinayak consoled himself with all sorts of arguments but could not achieve desired source of satisfaction.

3

Avadhesha sauntered along the paved path prevailing sea-waves from disturbing human habitations. There were seen people in twos & threes and some lonely walkers also.

He caught the aweful sight of the vast sea-waves escorted by sky-scrapers. Amazing juxtaposition of creativity of nature and human brain.

A faint memory of Irene arose in his sub-conscious. He vividly remembered her kisses on his cheeks in the Art-Gallery. He had made many abortive attempts to be in her contact.

Her behavior with him was beyond comprehension. It was rather mystifying. Her display of love for him was curiously short-lived. It was a kind of drifting away from him.

But why?

He could not locate any tangible and rational explanation. He glanced at the sea-scape and a kind of feeling gripped his mind.

Irene's beautiful face swam in his sub-conscious. His encounter with her in the Art-Gallery swept him like a sea-wave.

'I wish she were with me. We could have a new feelingful human aspect to the various visible aspects of nature.'

He heaved a deep sigh and became sensitively conscious of his morbid loneliness.

A few steps ahead on the pavement and he came across a girl staring at him.

'Sir, would you like to make a rant?'

'What do you mean?' he enquired rather peevishly.

'Look over there. You see two small gatherings. Ideas are dangerous' is the key-word to the fest. You can make a brief rant for two minutes. Please walk ahead and get your name registered.'

Avadhesha felt a sort of release from his painful loneliness. His throbbing in his nerves became less tense.

'Thank you very much.'

The girl responded with a faint smile. He proceeded towards the spot for registration of his name. He felt a kind of boost to his positive feeling and a release from mental anguish. After undergoing the process of registration he stepped towards the group. It was a small conglomeration of different nationalities.

The fest of the rant was in full swing. The managers of the rant were quite active and attentive to the proceedings of the event. A bell would ring after every two minute to draw the attention of the new speaker.

It was Avadhesha's turn like every other speaker. He stood on the pedestal and wasted his two minutes in introducing himself to the small audience. Then he remarked that civilization was primilarly a product of creative imagination attributed to peculiar cells of human brain.

Man can go for inventions and constructions. His brain is capable of imbibing abstractions and giving them tangible shapes.

There arose a shrill voice of the bell. Reluctantly he stepped down the pedestal and was questioned by a girl of the fest. The next speaker was a blonde with her naked flesh unroabed to the level of her breasts. All eyes were focused on her. She imparted a bewitehing smile to her face. A stray voice from among the audience vibrated, 'last year you performed something extra-ordinary in the fest!'

'Please, repeat the same.'

The small gathering was rather curious to know the feat of the last year. She opened her lips and multered rather cynically—

'Oh, my God. You still remember the trick I played last year.

'It was more of spirituality than physicality.'

Another voice vibrated in the atmosphere—'We are much interested in your spirituality.'

'Please, repeat the trick.'

All stood dumb-founded for the grand spectacle. It did not materialize. A wave of dismay swept through the audience.

However the lady spoke something regarding evolution. She did not make any reference to Darwin's evolution.

She did not make a mention of 'Origin of Species'.

Her rant followed a dismayed clapping. They were interested in the spectacles of flesh denied to them.

The last speaker to step on the pedestal was an Indian. In a typical Indian accent he spoke about Gandhi's performance in India.

'Gandhi's non-voilent movements and love of truth became the most potent instruments in the hands of fragile human being who gave India the required deliverance from the yoke of British imperialism.

'Gandhi was interested neither in science, nor in literature. He was interested only in human beings. That is why we killed him.'

A quote from Aldous Huxley's Ape and Essence swam into Avadhesha's memory.

The event was coming towards a close.

Results were declared followed by intermetant clappings. Every participant was given a certificate recommending his participation in the event.

Avadhesha again started fuming and fretting at his loneliness. 'Without human touch life is really a lonely journey. It is insipid and without any flavor. Why not to go for a glass of beer?'

He entered the primesis of a bar. Before entering the bar, he gave an intensive glance to the sprawling sea-waves tossing their heads. They bore the burden of two visible ships and many boats.

Avadhesha inwardly was pining for the presence of Irene. He looked up the sky bare to the nooks and corners.

The British poet, Wordsworth was enamored of such sights of nature. In the bar he bought a glass of beer and seated himself on a cornered seat.

A glass of beer stood before him at the table. He had a sip of beer and a woman came in and seated herself on sofa.

She sat facing him.

'A nice rant you made, 'Were you in the group?'

'O Yes, yes but you led yourself into your introduction.'

'The count of time slipped my mind. Only two minutes for the rant. Hardly any time to express even a fraction of yourself.'

'True, true but there are limits. Quite a good number of speakers.'

She started munching something. Avadhesha looked at her casually. Her face was not even. she was a bit bulky.

Avadhesha muttered to himself,—'The bar is rather expensive.'

The woman in front of him nodded her assent and spoke in a husky voice,—'it's expensive. Look outside the premises. What a rich repast of nature! Surroundings matter. It's away from the usual hum drum of life. You know what matters are the surroundings. The atmosphere is tranquil and away from the humdrum of life.'

Avadhesha spilled draughts of beer inside him. He continued the conversation. Another woman joined the conversation.

Avadhesha cast an intimate glance at her. Her features looked quite peculiar, away from the features of an ordinary woman. He was glad to be in the female company.

'When did you come back from Russia?'

'A month back.'

'Where are your husband and children?'

'At home.'

'You came without them from Ukrain to Sydney?'

'It's simply amazing.'

So far Avadhesha had not uttered any word. Yes, there was something fascinating about the woman.

Conversation should have a beginning. Then it comes to an end itself.

'So you belong to the land of Tolstoy?' Avadhesha butted in his words. Suddenly she raised her eyes-lids with a faint smile on her face. Her eye-lids encompassed the facial contours of Avadhesha.

'Yes, I belong to the land of Tolstoy and many other great writers.'

Avadhesha was bent upon displaying his intimate familiarity with Russian authors. He spoke like an erudite,' 'Crime and Punishment' is the novel going into the area of split personality.'

'O! You seem to be quite intimately familiar with the whole lot. Tolstoy's 'War and Peace' captures the concept of timelessness into bonds of time.

'Yes that's true.' The woman uttered her words.

'What an panoramic novel it is? Napolean's invasion of Russia!

Russians defeated his attacks on their country.

Fascinating!

'And Dr. Zivago?'

Avadhesha came out with a quote from Dr. Zivago—'Art is occupied with two unending, constant occupations. On the one hand it is concerned with the problem of death; on the other hand, it is creating a new life.'

The lady was highly impressed and spoke with full eloquence, 'You! from which country?'

'From India. Visiting Sydney.'

'Visiting Sydney?'

'Yes.'

'Your awareness about Russian authors is quite amazing.

'We have Puskin's statue in front of shahitya Academy, New Delhi. Every year writers from India visit Russia. They are given free passage, boarding and lodging.'

'You know more about Russian authors than I know.'

Avadhesha did not respond with any significant expression to the lady's remarks.

He peeped outside through the glass window and espied a heavy conglomeration of scattered clouds.

They constituted a pattern of roof of some grand building.

Avadhesha was extremely impressed by the sway of clouds. He glanced intensely at the bosom of the sea-waves, supporting boats and ships.

'Is it not a painting painted by God?'

The word 'painting' reminded him of Irene. She must be deciphering paintings for visitors. She has eloquence in her voice. It rings sweet to the psyche of the listeners.

She casts a shadow of beauty whenever she walks or talks. Emotions free a man from the mundane hum-drum of life and paints rosy pictures of human beings and objects. Human preceptivion is seldom detached and objective.

It is colored by the feelings and the environment of the movement. That movement collapses giving place to another psychological hue.

What a quick succession of movements and their myriad manifestation!

Avadhesha withdrew his peeping to find the two women gone from the pub. He did not even hear the rustle of their departure.

'Lovers have left without leaving their addresses.' He began to gulp the last remannants of beer. He was reminded of T.S eliot's 'The Waste Land'

His sudden loneliness was a matter of somekind of mental discomfort.

4

It was not just a drive in the car for Ram and his father. It was a sort of pilgrimage for them as they were heading towards Iscon temple situated in north Sydney. Ram's father is on three month's visit to Sydney. Since his arrival in the metropolis he has been craving for a visit to some Indian religious place. Again and again he would tell his son, 'No Krishna here, No Rama here?'

'This city is of full of only physical charms, well-dressed boys, girls, men, women walking in a big hurry. That's why I was reluctant to visit Sydney!'

Ram time and again assured his father, 'Father, don't worry, Sydney is full with spots of all religions.'

It is crowded with churches, temples, gurudwaras and mosques. Every community has religious spots and is given complete freedom to handle them in accordance with their religious beliefs. They are allowed to have their rituals and ceremonies without disturbing the general flow of humanity.

The father was much excited and amazed at the prospect of visiting lord Krishna. At this moment the sky was studded with half formed moon.

The city was crowded with neon-lights. The stars had receded in feebleness because of the flood of the man made lights. The trees were the only evidence left of the vast planet. They stood tranquil and unconcerned.

The car was running through a long tunnel fully illuminated with electric bulbs and tubes. Ram's father felt almost bewildered at the infrastructure of Sydney.

'How do you feel, father?'

'Just amazed, beautiful roads, no crowds, no rush on roads, simply amazing!'

The termination of the tunnel ushered them into an area of thick inter-twined trees and a steady flow of the sea in the vicinity of the road.

'I feel proud that our Lord Krishna lives in this city of beauty. Our Krishna is mighty and omnipresent. He can travel anywhere he likes. The entire universe belongs to him.'

Ram was quite happy to hear his father talking like this. At least he would not resent the money he has spent on Sydney fare.

Next visit his mother too will come. Ram thought the trees on the roadside were under a slight windy sway as soon as they reached the temple. Ram's father bowed his head in gratitude to Lord Krishna.

They went inside the temple and seated themselves near the statue of lord Krishna. The room was almost crowded. Ram's father was delighted to find white skinned men and women among the devotees. They had put on *tilacks* on their foreheads and were chanting—

'Hare Krishna, Hare Krishna, Hare Rama, Hare Rama, Hare, Hare.'

'It is astonishing for me to see many *goras* in the temple. Today I understand Lord Krishna is present everywhere. He resides in every particle of the universe. He lives in the hearts of all human beings.'

The chanting of the mantra was in crescendo. It was accompanied by drum beating and mild dancing. Men, women, boys, girls were under the impact of musical sway.

Their feet moved in unison to and fro. They were in a vibrate contract of God's praise being distilled through chanting of hymns.

Ram's father was immediately under the magical impact of incantations being resounded in the inner room of the temple.

'Hare Krishna, Hare Rama' swam like glow worms in the premises of the temple. Some devotees conversed in whispers. Outside the auditorium stood a shop selling books, ornaments, garlands, replicas and many other articles connected with Lord Krishna. Some devotees were busy scanning the pages of books. Ram's father was highly impressed. In India a casual impression is that Indian religions are being distorted and made fun of in foreign countries.

No, it is misleading.

White-skinned ladies dressed as *gopies*!

Simply bewitching to look at them.

Indian attires. some of them had protruding bosoms but Ram's father withdrew his looks lest he should into the ditch of sin and duly punished in his next birth.

Now it is time for *Artee* and chanting with bowed heads and a sharp increase in the sound of chanting. Ram's father came to know something extraordinary about Prabhupad ji.

He was astonished to look at his statue as he had never heard of him.

'*Prsadam* is to be bought' Ram whispered into the ears of his father.

'What the hell do you mean?

Langars (free distribution of food) are common in our country.' Ram's father was reluctant to buy '*Prsadam*' (food) from lord Krishna's temple.

'He is a feeder of all humanity. He would be angry if we paid him for '*Prsadam*'.

'His kingdom is vast and he provides food to all the creatures of the universe.

'I'll not eat bought *Prsadam*.'

'Bapu, do not angry and annoyed. They can't afford to provide free food to everyone.'

Ram tried to persuade his father.

Bapu responded, 'O.K I don't mind.'

'I feel like visiting toilet.'

'Come, come Bapu. I lead you to the toilet.'

Ram left his father at the entrance of the toilet and withdrew from there. Bapu's eye-lids began to flutter.

'Lo . . . . look . . . a *gopi* in the arms of a young man.'

'Hellish ! sinful ! all *gopies* belong to lord Krishna and to no one else. He is the supreme master and lord of everything on this planet.'

White urinating, he was fuming and fretting. He muttered to himself, 'It is not sacred. A *gopi* in the arms of an ordinary boy? Her place is with the celestial being, lord Krishna.'

On his way back, he thought of revealing every detail to Ram. But in India, it is not to have such talks with sons and daughters.

So the best is to keep quiet and pray to Krishna to take care of his *gopies*.

It was ten O' clock in the night.

Ram and his father came back from the temple. They were in a mood of devotion to lord Krishna.

Ram was on the night duty. He handed over the keys of the apartment to Bapu and proceeded towards the destination of his duty.

Bapu thought it better to sit in a small park located in the front of a pub.

It is since long that he sat in the open to look at the vast sky.

In India, in his village he was often working in his fields. He got ample opportunity to suck in fresh air. He seated himself on a vacant bench. Another man was also seated on the same bench.

Bapu looked at him intently but received almost no response and any urge to talk to him.

In his village in India he was often in the company of fellow-farmers sharing *Hukka* (a smoking device in India).

Smoking *Hukka* often accompanied a lot of laughter and gossips embracing many aspects of the human life. There used to be kicks of laughter.

Bapu made an attempt to have some threads of conversation with the man sitting on the same bench. But the man on the bench shied away from talking and began to peer in the direction of the pub.

O! the Indian middle-aged man (Bapu) was bewildered to see a beautiful woman standing at the entrance of the pub. A queue of men of all ages.

'But to what purpose?'

Bapu intensified his gaze at the woman in order to decipher the spectacle. She was being implanted kisses by men standing in the queue.

It was the rarest sight for Bapu. It gave to him a moral shock beyond measure. He shrugged his shoulders and said to himself, 'My god, Ram lives in such a land. He is likely to get his character impaired and his fall is inevitable.'

The man sitting next to him was feeling a bit tipsy. Suddenly he gave a push to himself and joined the queue.

Bapu kept on looking constantly in the direction of the pub. His eyes were blinking. After the lapse of 15 minutes the Australian came back to the bench.

He looked at the fellow-bencher and spoke to him in slow moving English.

'Why don't you go and kiss the girl? It is quite relishing.'

He moved his lips in the manner of kissing.

Bapu could not make out the full purport of the old man's promptings. But he would guess that he wanted him to go to the girl and kiss her.

Bapu fell into a net-work of conflicts. His instinct prompted him to go and taste the lips of the girl.

But a strong morality persuaded him to the contrary. The girl was just like his daughter-in-law. But it was a rarer opportunity. It was a god-sent opportunity to taste the lips of another female.

The man on the bench spoke to him, 'What are you lost in? Go and kiss the girl.'

'It is a free event. The girl will slip away.'

Bapu's imagination ran wild. He thought that Ram's mother couldn't think of this situation. He was absolutely an unknown figure here. He had no score of earning a bad name or caught.

In his own village in India such opportunities are beyond the reach of a common man. He visualized of his village women with pitchers on their heads going to village wells.

They make it a point to cover their heads. If at all they peep it is through their aprons with shy and withdrawing looks.

Bapu got worried about his own moral character. It created a sort of dilemma in his sub-conscious.

'The girl will go away. What's your problem? Go and kiss the girl.'

The Australian was amused at Bapu.

He suddenly stood up and went for another bench. He sat on the bench and started mumbling *mantras*. His lips moved in a rapid crecendo uttering something known only to him.

The tipsy Australian was watchful of him and thought him to be a quaint man. After the collapse of some moments, he proceeded towards the pub with massive moral hassals.

He joined the queue and waited for his turn. The girl looked at him with a quaint dim smile. He kissed on her left cheek rather apologetically and fled the scene as soon as possible.

5

Avadhesha got down the stairs in the casino. The sun was about to set in the dimming sun rays across the vast sky. It was a slow ushering in the empire of the evening.

Lights were on illuminating the stairs and other vicinities. Avadhesha came down, ignored the salutation of the taxi-drivers and preferred to follow a solitary path.

He was feeling grief-stricken time and again.

Yes, Irene had swum to his sub-conscious with full emotional contours. It was there despite human rationally. Human mind is full of impulses, emotions, intuitions and neurosis. It is constantly in a state of influx, consisting of moods and streaks of submerged thoughts. He crossed the road and proceeded in the direction of sea-shore. He craved for loneliness to console his mind on Irene's remembrance.

After crossing a few zigzag turns of the road he occupied a cemented bench. His glance flashed in several directions.

In the hazy nook and corners of the sea-shore he could dimly see lovers lost in each other's arms. His gaze stayed at the flat sea surges that did not show any irregular movement.

With the dawn of the evening the sea takes a gruesome aspect.

Why did Irene kiss him?

It might be out of sheer physical sensation but for him it became an emotional obsession. He started pining for Irene not for physicality, more for emotional satisfaction.

There was some emotion in her kisses and some streaks of sentiments. How could he share his feeling with someone?

There is none known to him in Sydney. His anguished soul craves sharing. In his own country he has many to console his anguished soul but here people are distanced from him. How could he lighten his emotional weight to the members of his family? It is stircktly against Indian traditions to share such feelings with them. It is highly a private affair confined to one's own self. The evening was transforming itself into night. The sea lay before him like a vast empire not absolutely mute and lonely.

The sea-waves resembled marching of civilizations.

Avadhesha's mutilated consciousness seized upon an idea. Why not to buy a woman in a brothel?

What is so unique about Irene?

The next moment his consciousness flew into a new direction. In a brothel he could not buy intensity, joy of relationship, beauty of soul and creativity. It is quite different with Irene. Her words echoed in his mind, 'So I take you to the empire of India. The empire synthesizes beauty with spiritually. Buddha in trance and other sculptures reflect eternal traditions of Indian culture.' Her words had poured like a fall of fresh water. He spoke to himself rather blantely, 'How can you heap the blame on her? She has different cultural roots. A different attitude to emotions. Quite possible she is not much sentimental. May be she loves a boy of her own country. True, true but why am I haunted by her?'

He began to stroll the sea-shore.

'Lo . . . .' he addressed himself, 'a crescent moon rises out of the deep sea. We are lost in our private sorrows and problems but nature is busy with the presentations of her own spectacles, often mute and regular spectacles run away from hum-drum that man has created for himself. Invariably they are placid but sometimes devastating. Human consciousness is a paltry drama against the endlessness of nature. Then why don't you forget Irene?'

It gave a bit of respose to his nerves. An expression of relief presided over his face. The other day he had come across Irene in the library. He was rather amazed to find her there. He had received a kind of boost and elevation to his sentiments.

'Irene, you here?'

'So, you recognize me. That's good. I thought you have forgotten me . . .'

Without finishing her sentence she moved at the back of the counter. There was a lot of freshness on her face. Her lips and eyes carried a unique sensitivity.

Her dress was immaculate and expression on her face was washed up.

He proceeded towards her.

'Oh, no, I can't talk. I am on duty. O.K?'

Her words betrayed a sort of harshness. She did not acknowledge his presence in a special manner. He was allowed to nourish his own mental anguish. Her words betrayed a sort of harshness. It resulted in an emotional set-back to Avadhesha.

He kept on looking at her sensitive face and contours of prettiness. He felt a terrible passionate fascination for her, but her forbidden looks betrayed something contrary to his expectation.

He was amazed and disillusioned and at a loss to understand the existing human situation. His chance meeting with Irene was culminating in a network of nothingness. He had been pining for her like a thirsty bird for water.

'Water, water everywhere nor any drop to drink.'

Literature is contexual to life and is kind of counterpart.

The library was humming with visitors. It was a grand spectacle of books being returned and issued.

Irene and her colleagues were lost in the routine of the library. It was routine process of books issued and returned.

Irene did not attach any importance to his presence in the library. He was left to his own speculations.

How should I talk to her? How would I pour my feelings to her? Oh, no, she was the same. It was a different aspect of her personality that choked his sub-conscious. She did not even look at him.

He picked up the current issue of Daily Telegraph and tried to draw himself in the pages of the news-paper.

'Why should not I read Crainer's zodice fore-cast?'

May be he has suggested some solutions to his mental dilemma!

No, it was not there.

Human emotions are no less volcanic—the explosions of bombs. Once or twice he looked at her but she seemed to be completely oblivious of his existence. In him grew a passionate, morbid longing to be with her.

'O god ! what a mental torture!'

What volcanic eruptions in his sub-conscious? A compulsive obsession that would engulf his mind to the brim.

He dared not go near her. An official expression sat on her face. Intermittently her colleagues conversed with her. Then she will be surrounded by library visitors. He went near the counter, but she avoided looking at him.

On the sea-shore Avadhesha suddenly caught snatches of conversation of a couple.

'You are refreshing, joy to kiss you, embrance you, hug you and then proceed further. I am glad to go ahead. Absolutely sensual, intoxicating.

When you penetrated deep into me, I forgot everything. Almost a trance Ecstasy.'

Snatches of conversation within the audible range of Avadhesha.

For a few moments his mental pain achieved some respite. 'That is not my pattern of relationship with Irene.' Avadhesha talked to himself alone. It was deep and emotion oriented that led to beauty, spirituality and at last physicality.

'Yes, I must write a novel. He suggested to himself loudly. It would be amazing escape or confrontation with his present predicament. O God! what a predicament!'

Who claims that human nature is ration and predictable? O, not the least. Human mind has many hidden corners. These are diverse and can not easily be made tangible. He again muttered to himself. A passing woman was held up for a moment, she fell into the illusion that he was addressing her.

A linger! and then she sped away from him. There are tall trees banking the sea-shore. These leaves were swaying in accordance with the direction and speed of the wind. These looked like watchmen of eternity. In a moment of flash, Avadhesha was reminded of Wordsworth, a great singer of nature. Alas! he is dead but nature is alive and extermely curious. What a paradox! He made desperate efforts to relieve himself of tension connected with Irene's neglect of him. His only fault, he mused is his intense love for her. She gives a blunted response to him.

Before the closing of the library he had stepped towards her and looked at her. Her face wore a stern expression.

He was quite scared of her. He summoned some courage and spoke to her in a husky voice, 'How should I express my heart to you? It's beyond me to express. It's beyond me to converse with you in the native language of my heart.'

Her reply to him was rather a blanket, 'you are just a client in the library and nothing else. Don't go beyond the decencies of normal behaviour. I work in the library and it's a public place.'

'Strange!' Avadhesha recalled the entire sequence of the Art-Galery. She had showered kisses on him in the croud. It was not a lonely human spot. He time and again questioned himself and was shell-shocked at the behavior of the lady.

'Why did she change herself?'

No reason, no rationality, no, nothing tangible. The same lady was now inmical, neutral to all his advances.

'I have starting writing a novel.' He had tried to impress her with his talent of writing.

'I'm not interested. I don't crave to be in your novel. Don't try to portray me. I warn you.'

Avadhesha was lost in zigzag of confusion at his recollections. Self-pity overwhelmed him.

'I think it's time to depart. The library is almost deserted. I can't converse with you anymore.'

She gave a refreshing smile at him and stepped out of the threshhold of the library and did not look back. She was surrounded by her colleagues. Avadhesha felt senseless and opaque to all hope. It was like a blind lane without a dim lamp lit at its corner. The moonlight in front of the skyscape was emerging like a thin pale reservoir of light with its rays scattered and embroided in the sea-waves. Gradually these were growing restive as massive blows of wind came into existence. These sea-waves gradually grew wild with the gravitational pull of the moon. An unknown terrior of the wild started taking shape in his sub-conscious. He hurried back with obstructed steps towards human habitation.

6

Trees on the sea-shore were already in the grip swaying gushes of wind. Avadhesha's face displayed a quick succession of many hues. It registered different feelings but Irene occupied the central situation in his mind.

She operated upon his vital brain cells. He threw a departing glance at the restive sea-waves. To him everything appeared mysterious.

A vast spectacle of Nature's immensity!

The trees banking the sea-shore appeared like ghosts and shadows. He kept on casting to and fro glances at the essentials of the sea-scape. These grew all the more uncanny and mysterious to him.

Suddenly a question took vivid shape in his contemplation.

Why does not Irene respond to his feelings?

He invariably finds her in her cheerful mood. She hardly shows any grimness on her face. It is certainly different and unusual.

She is not in a hurry to explain herself. On the other hand she maintains her usual self. Perhaps what matters are the cultural background, genes and environment responsible for his growth.

He addressed himself rather harshly, 'Everyone is not like you. Emotions are topsy turvey. Everyone is different and has his own mental-makeup, genes.'

He found a kind of shelter for Irene's response to him. This kind of rationalization did not create a balanced attitude in him.

He sheltered himself in a café and felt relieved of his emotional burden and was glad to be away from the wilderness of the sea.

'Man has to protect himself.' He murmured to himself in prophetic tones.

There were many customers in the café. It was a lot of relief to Avadhesha in the presence of other human beings. He found a kind of security in the café.

'A regular capphichino.' he politely spoke to the woman at the counter and handed over three dollars to her. She uttered a ritualistic thanks to him.

Two pretty girls sat in the nearby chairs.

Most of Sydney girls are well-dressed and pretty. He thought to himself. He sipped the first draught of coffee and got some mental relief.

The two girls were engaged in talking to each other and were sharing the pleasure of this movement. Their eyes did not show any random movement.

Avadhesha was trying his best to expand his inner cheerfulness. He strongly wished to escape the dark cave of grief. The word grief reminded him of the Russian author Anton Chekov's short-story. 'Grief' The cab driver lost his son to the sinister jaws of death. His overwhelming grief strained at sharing. But none was there to listen to his unhappy tale of his son's death. All his attemps to draw attention to his grief were foiled. The little cab, by the everything was steaming stamping. He was lead to his horse and narrated to the animal the sad incidence of his son's death.

Like the cabman he uttered dimly—

'To whom should I tell my grief?'

In the café Avadhesha was apart from it.

He posed a question to himself, 'Why do you love Irene so intensely?'

She belongs to a foreign strand and cultural make-up. Even then such a persistent, blind, massive longing and craving for her?

Intense remembrance for her render him so sad and listless!

But why? why?

Time and again he demanded a rational explanation from his inner-self.

There was neither an explanation nor any rationality for his craving for Irene.

Moreover she seems to care a fig for him. She gives to him the impression of being quite unrelated sways like a mighty stream in him.

The café was lit with brilliant lights. He suddenly made up his mind to smoke.

'Why?'

Whenever he feels emotionally topsy he smokes. It proves to be an oasis in the vast desert of sand.

He left the café and entered the nearby smoking zone. He squatted on a chair and lit a cigarette. His face yielded the impression of some intencine conflict of his sub-conscious.

'Why this intense craving for Irene? Has it some connection with some past events lost in her unconscious. Did he ever feel blind passion for someone in the past that keeps smouldering in the inner layers of his mind?'

He imparted a wide awake yawning to his mind.

'Yes' there did exist a girl in his childhood.

Yes, what was her name?

Yes it was Smiriti a student of class ninth studying with him in the same class. Unknowingly she was drawn towards him. Her words echoed in his mind at the present moment of silent smoking.

'Never drift away from me, Avadhesha. My love for you is blind and pure.' He had taken her in his arms.

Their breathing was in perfect unison. It was deep, profound and heart-rendering. He recollects they were wrapt in each other like two vipers.

'Avadhesha, never think of your existence apart from me. Look at the setting sun and rising stars. Let us make the moment eternal.'

Avadhesha's tears were flowing like spontanious falls from the pure earth.

'Don't you worry dear Smiriti. God has created us to merge into each other. If you believe in rebirth we are related in some way.'

And then Smiriti had started caressing his black hair pressing his head to her growing breasts.

Her blooming breasts had softly embraced him. May be his love for Irene is off. Shoot of the past regressions come to one's subconscious. It is an unfathomed reservoir of memories conflicts, unsatisfied instincts.

Powerful dramas live in our sub-merged selves.

'Why shouldn't I forget Irene and throw her into oblivion?' There are women and women in the world. Is she extra talented?'

But her grip over his mind and emotions is potent and mind-boggling. It has penetrated deep in his nerves.

The more he tries to emancipate himself from her, the more she sinks into the inner blind caves of his mind.

He just could not push himself out of this emotional, slippery ground. Irene maintained her sweet indifference towards him.

To begin with, she was soft towards him. But now she stood like a rock of some ancient mountain.

7

Dawning in Sydney shows multifarious aspects. If you look at the sky, some stars continue shining very brightly and some assume dim aspect and yet some proceed towards slow extinction.

Avadhesha has always been sensitive to the slow and headlong changes in nature.

To-day man has alienated himself from the raw, divine matter of nature and is aliening himself to technological systems of human soul and human sensitivity.

One fine morning he decides to be a regular visitor to the Uniting church, Rockdale, that stands in the close vicinity of his residence.

'Will it be possible for him to adjust with the diversities?'

Church is altogether a different approach to walk to the kingdom of God. To begin with, he feels a bit nervy regarding his resolve. But then a glimmer hope pushes him towards his decision.

On Sunday morning at 09:30 a.m he steps into church premises and finds himself surrounded by strangers. He is supposed to converse and hear everything in English.

To begin with, he feels isolated and segregated. He keenly attempts to listen to and understand whatever is being preached by the prelate, Rev. Martin.

It is a sheer delight and relish to listen to him. His communications are punctuated with hymns sung to the accompaniment of piano.

For Avadhesha it was difficult to keep place with the rhythm and rhythms of hymns sung during the services.

He was delighted to hear interpretations of christian scriptures. He was amazed to follow their contents nearly corresponding the contents of Hindu scriptures. No vital difference among the systems of different religions.

They embody the same human contents; a plea for love and compassion.

Then, what are the causes of conflicts among them?

These are the outcome of dogmas attached to them by some fanatics. It is indicative of their isolated, individual vanities. It is nothing but falsehood perpetuated by those keen to maintain their leadership and prominence.

Avadhesha often expresses his sentiments to Martin and his wife Margret. They are glad to hear him. Avadhesha is glad at heart to win the approval of his ideas from the leading man of the church.

Martin's face does not display any diplomacy or intrigue. In his expressive response he is candid like a transparent glass.

To begin with, he was led to the suspicion that he might not integrate himself with the system. But with the passage of time his false fears and apprehensions slipped away through the gate of death.

Slowly he gained familiar behavior of the christian community in the church.

'Compassion' is a singular word imparting dignity and summing up to the parables and religious contexts from 'The Bible'

There is hardly any observance of any rituals in the proceedings of the service in church.

The context of the serman is of the paramount importance of practical virtues aimed at the betterment of life.

There is hardly any mythology involved in the preaching of the service.

'Compassion' is the singular word that sums up the entire serman and imparts dignity to the entire structure of the sermon.

In the bigger hall of the church we come across a gathering of multicultural community.

Their conversations with one another are varied and interesting. Avadhesha is keen to talk to the attractive and beautiful girls hailing from divergent countries.

It is a thrilling experience to cast our glances and then be in contract with different men, women, boys and girls.

For Avadhesha it was sometimes very different to understand Australian accent in English. He felt bewildered and puzzled as he was conscious of his hold on English. His way of English was typically Indian. One day, in the church, an old lady spoke to him in English.

She spoke in soft tones, 'Avadhesha, please speak a bit slowly. Difficult to understand your English.'

He felt surprised, puzzled and confused.

He longed to say something to the lady.

Their conversation did not run a smooth path. They paused many a time to fill up gaps in language. The old lady seemed to be a bit dissatisfied with him.

'It's difficult to make up what you say.' And she gave a definite jerk to her neck and turned away the gaze of old, blue eyes. Her lids were fluttering at the sudden growth of this situation.

Avadhesha muttered to himself. It is not deliberate rejection of my company but my genuine complication in communication.

He found himself mentally isolated from the inmates present in the hall.

Should he stop visiting church?

'No, no,' . . .he vehemently spoke to himself. Church is the place of Christ. Moreover he gets the feel of international community.

How could Martin surmise his troubled state of mind?

He up-lifted his eye-brows and found Martin facing him with a kind smile on his face. It was an outcome of human feeling for him.

'Avadhesha, aren't you feeling alright today?'

'O, no . . . I am not feeling anything bad, at times Australian accent of English troubles me. I find it difficult to bridge small gaps in the flow of conversations.'

Martin took hold of his hand and gave consolation to him.

'You can talk your heart to me.' Martin's eloquence gave a new stream of blood slot to the receding spirits of Avadhesha's psyche.

Suddenly Martin's wife Margret swims into his mental-ken. She is growing in age yet retaining the vital beautiful remants of her prime youth. She beams at Avadhesha and he picks up her sagging spirits.

Her soul feels like a king of flutter oozing in him new enthusiasm. It is more or less a sublime elevation.

For an Artist or a writer the other sex always plays a vital role.

It is a kind of stirring, a kind of stimulation at least for a man with artistic temperament.

'The other woman'—these words go deep in to the artist's psyche. These strings carry an emotional chat for him. It is like the outline of a story that can be filled in with human situations and content.

At times he looks into Margret's eyes and feels a kind of emotion away from love. He shakes hands with her.

A smile greets him.

'How are you today Avadhesha?'

Her flashing eye-lids and peculiar kiss gives an immense satisfaction to Avadhesha.

One day after the culmination of services in church Avadhesha was followed by a Chinese woman. She yelled for him to stop.

He looked back and found Chang asking him to stop. He was rather amazed with curiosity-stricken face. He lingered on for Chang's arrival.

'Chang, your company is always very interesting.'

'Avadhesha, you come with me.' She husked her words.

'Where?'

'To home.'

'Members of your family may not take it very kindly.

'I live alone.'

There was a big sparkle in her eyes.

'There are no members of family at home. The other day you talked to me about your son and daughter-in-law. It's claver of you to remember the details of our past conversation. You are exact to the point.'

'But what?'

Avadhesha gave a soft push to Chang to lead her to a sequestered spot in a corner of the veranda. He wanted to secure a sort of lonely atmosphere they could carry on private conversation. Chang bore a secret smile on her face.

Avadhesha looked at her mysteriously. Chang heaved a deep sigh of grief and whispered, 'As soon as I step into the house my daughter-in-law steps out of home and makes way to her parent's home who reside in the adjoining street.

'Strange! Very strange!'

Avadhesha too was a bit taken aback at their conduct.

'Why?'

'I don't know exactly. May be she does not like my looks or way of talking.'

'Your daughter-in-law is too foolish. I must say Chang; your looks are beyond your age. You have a slippery, docile face. Even then!'

'That's your opinion and not of my daughter-in-law. At times women are jealous of each other for nothing. Just for the heck of it. It's good of you to console me. So nice of you. Thank you very much. It encourages me, the only ray of hope for me. At least I share my feelings with you.

'It's a great Indian virtue.

'I feel amazed!'

'Amazed! at what?'

Chang last cast a glance at the closing shutters of shops.

Bright lights in Sydney keep the shadows of darkness of the night lit thereby giving a semblance of optimism throbbing.

Even the deserted, less frequented roads become a kind of witness of human drama on foot.

Sometimes tall, well-spread trees spread their branches in full bloom and throw their patches partially or in totality. It is a lonely drama enacted by nature.

The stirrings of leaves on wide spread trees create ripples of vast magnitude and in the way are manipulated by myriad plastered walls and roads.

'Avadhesha, you seem to be lost somewhere?'

'O, nowhere!'

'You can't tell me blank lies. By the way, Avadhesha can you come with me home?'

'For what?'

'Just for chat. We shall talk our minds to each other. Now I am assured of one thing. Humans to whatever country they belong to are just the same. They are moved by the same propensities. Only they speak different languages and expressions and create different human situations in different countries. Consider your relationship with your daughter-in-law.'

'You are a Chinese woman but you speak of usual embroils at home. I simply wonder.'

They got engrossed in domestic hum-drum talks of without being aware of the constant flow of humanity. The procession of humanity on Sydney roads is rather thin.

Avadhesha was reminded of over-busy and over-crowded lanes and roads of cosmopolitan and other cities in his country.

How people jostle against one another? They feel pestered in many ways.

'Same in china' Chang gave a smile and spoke a bit louder. 'All over the world people face same calamities and have to manage themselves according to their different circumstances.

'We have different ways to govern country and our system is rather tough and quite strict. We don't have a democratic way of life. Our systems are rather different.'

Chang was no longer interested in furthering political agenda. She was interested in creating human situation with Avadhesha.

Avadhesha felt reluctant and handicapped because of the values he inherited from the land of his own culture. In his own country such head-long encounters are very rare and these take some time to settle down.

Head-long romantic situations are invariably seen in Indian movies.

In such encounters society steps in. Otherwise the movie does not follow the usual beaten path of social embroils and conflicts. The family dramatic conflict is an inevitable sequence.

Otherwise romantic situation is thrown into an isolation. And this kind of romantic isolation is not a part of Indian psyche. They remain incompleted until trapped by social circumstances.

Chang uttered a sentence with a prolonged smile.

'You are feeling amazed. I am not asking you for a marriage bond. I am in for a petty chat. Let's have some cold drinks. O.K, what would you like to have? Please name the drink!'

She had preference for diet coke and the same was consumed by Avadhesha himself.

They consumed it rather slowly in order to prolong their association on the road side.

Avadhesha was thinking that countries and places don't make any vital or basic difference. It is just the same.

Chang had enough appeal for Avadhesha. Her fingers held the same fascination for him as he would feel for any Indian girl. The Chinese aroused an enormous curiosity. He felt rather flattered that he was followed by a Chinese girl.

A lovely female structure to capture anyone's imagination.

May be one day he squeezes her in his arms and feels the universal excitement of sex.

An imaginary stimulation thrills the vital of his body charging him for an instant intense emotional experience.

He builds up his castles about chang. Strange he did not feel pangs of guilt. The cultural milieu in this country allows this kind of diversity.

They do not stick to one woman. Variation is allowed to both the sexes.

As in India, it does not fall into the area of sin. It is considered as good as human instincts. They do not suffocate themselves in pangs of guilt and suppression imposed by an unknown entity.

Avadhesha thought constantly and deeply.

Is it not man made?

Yes, in fact both the sexes are polygamist. Variety is the real joy of life. But it is certainly against Indian way of life.

Here relationship between husband and wife is not loosely knit. Invariably it extends to seven births and deaths.

It is a cyclic relationship going around and paving way to an abiding unity of the two souls.

They start recognizing each other without their body being governed by unknown forces. It is simply miraculous and wonderful.

Avadhesha and chang bade good-bye to each other. It was afternoon. The flow of humanity on the road was unabated and disciplined. There was hardly any noise pollution. Avadhesha thought of lanes and roads of his own country.

Even walking is not safe. There is seldom any relief or respite to traffic. Even narrow lanes are crowded with two wheelers and these appear like glow worms.

It is so sudden and unexpected that they seem to be rushing over your body. At their disappearance we have a sign of relief. But they rush on not paying even an iota of attention to the safety of pedestrians.

Avadhesha saw chang disappear on the road. Suddenly Avadhesha cast a glance at the vast sky spread before him like a vast canvass of painting. It was jolted with several patches of clouds sneaking out of their hidden abodes.

It was a grand spectacle. The blue sky above and the man-made infrastructure glimmering in the same sun-shine.

Avadhesha felt a wave of excitement passing through the vitals of his body, mind and soul.

He was reminded of another engagement in the company of Martin Bishop of Uniting church.

Avadhesha thought that he must undergo various experiences to fully understand the moral, cultural nuisances of a country.

There are differences which may shock us beyond our measure. These may invade the sanctity of many of our long-life concepts dear to our thinking, practice and philosophy of life.

Avadhesha was at Martin's house exactly at 9 o'clock to join the small group to visit a nursing home for the aged.

He was much excited because the purpose of visiting any new place or situation was something of extra interest to him.

Martin greeted him with a smile beyond his whiskers. He led him inside his inhabitat. Quite neat, clean house full of books of all times and different subjects. The house was completely modern in out-look and equipment.

He did not show any hospitality to Avadhesha, quite baffling to him. His Indian notions of hospitality received a hurt.

Not even a glass of water!

May be it's a part of Sydney culture!

May be they do not believe these formalities. Unlike Indians they do not indulge in these small acrobatics.

Martin led Avadhesha to his car and they occupied the front seat. It was a drive of half an hour. A crowdless road lay before him.

Spick and span traffic in strict discipline.

Avadhesha was highly impressed. Mammoth crowds in his own country send a sensation through his spinal cords.

O god! What crowds?

No traffic rules. Sometimes it is a jungle of noises. All sorts of noises. Sounds of horns. Zigzag traffic! Endless vehicles speeding on the verge of collusion.

Some roads littered with dirty garbage. Avadhesha was simply stunned at the differences of infrastructure of the two countries.

Infrastructure of a country lends something new and beautiful to the country. It is an integral part of the environment of a country.

Suddenly Martin slowed down the car and took right turn. A few steps ahead and there stood the nursing home for the aged.

'A neat and clean space. Martin, it's simply fascinating. The surroundings are ideal and captivating.' Avadhesha blurted out and Martin's bearded face wore a faint smile.

'It's nice of you to talk like that.'

'I couldn't help speaking like that. Something stays with me, a kind of excitement! Assortment of sensations!'

'Highly emotional!'

Martin uttered feebly.

In front in the sky the moon of the morning lay half-dead.

The sky bore a sort of placidity bereft of all clouds.

Avadhesha's feet were in unison following the impact of the atmosphere.

'Let's walk in.' Martin led Avadhesha to the interior of the nursing home. A few paved patches of floor embedded with grass and plants.

And then a long winding corridor studded with a number of doors leading to the central room. A common room meant for the meeting of the aged in the habitat. Neat and clean. Everything well arranged in the wide space of the room.

Avadhesha received a kind of mental set-back at the sight of brooding inmates of the room.

O god, its mysterious. Yes, a deep mystery. This human life. Its origin and termination.

Avadhesha gave a stretch to his imagination and visualized the earlier youthful years of the aged.

They must have been quick, romantic and full of vigor lost in the waves of their dreams. But now they are in state of vacancy—a void that can never be refilled.

Avadhesha's eyes were wet. But who can escape this?

None of us. Avadhesha was reminded of T.S Eliot's poem-'The Hallowmen, and a few lines flashed in his sub-conscious—

'Between idea and action there falls a shadow. Between conception and creation there falls a shadow.

'We are hallow men. We wear the bottoms of our trousers rolled. Where is the life, we have lost in living?'

The central room was spaced with unusual quiet.

A search of futility in human life. The aged sit in groups of twos and threes and stare at one another without conveying anything substantial. In fact they had nothing to express. One of them leaned forward and addressed Martin, 'Do you recognize me? I am Sam, you remember a player of some re-known. I was a well known sportsman.'

His lips twitched, his eye-lids blinked without any control of reflexes.

Martin beamed a smile on his face and nodded to him in full smile. There was a kind of extinguish in his eyes and spoke, 'Once I talked to you romantic stuff. Don't you recollect?'

'Oh, yes . . . . most vividly.'

There arose a squeaking yell from another old man. The nurses ran toward him, examined his complete body.

His eyes looked at his face but could not maintain the stare at her. Martin asked Avadhesha to distribute extracts and hymns from the Bible printed on large papers. Some of them smiled.

The extracts from the Bible gave consolation to them.

Martin meanwhile, began to chant the contents in a melodious voice. More voices followed the singing. Many lips came in slow movements and were repetitive too. Avadhesha felt it a little trying to sing the accents of some words. It took the forms of a chorus led by the lonely singing of the prelate.

Avadhesha's eyes wandered from one face to another and then looked at the faces of young nurses. It was something refreshing for him. He stared at them a bit longer than required. Their faces looked spiritually fresh and in tune and gave glimpses of their hearts and minds. He wished to converse with them.

But what?

Their dedication to the aged was beyond doubt. The chorus was in progress in unison but with some obstructed voices.

Some of the aged could not sing properly and their words evaporated into whispers. Avadhesha was led into a mood of contemplation. We humans face the same destiny of extinction, country, religion, language, cultures and everything else related to human life is terminated by death.

It has uniformity and asserts itself as the law of nature.

Avadhesha felt awed by looking at the decayed faces and registered a sensation of despair. Martin whispered to Avadhesha.

'Let's go. Let's not disturb them more. They have to follow their routine.'

An elderly lady appeared at the door. She gave a broad smile to Martin and spoke, 'Service is over. Could you console them?'

Martin quipped, 'Oh yes, oh yes, it is always consoling and full of mental comfort.'

The lady spoke in a quick tone, 'Oh, yes, thank you very much for your visit.'

She turned her inquisitive look at Avadhesha.

Martin spoke in candid tones, 'He is Avadhesha from india. Visiting sydney'

'Fine. Most welcome. How do you feel about your visit?

'Oh! It's wonderful and refreshing. It's a new experience to be here.'

'That's fine,' the lady too replied.

Avadhesha handed over the lady two copies of his novel, 'Twilight.'

Martin patted Avadhesha's shoulder, 'He is the author of the novel.'

Avadhesha imparted a humble nod to the lady.

'Thank you very much. I'm glad to have your books. A good gift to the library. Here some like to read books.'

Avadhesha was glad to hear words but felt a bit bewildered, and then spoke with a bit of hesitation, 'Do they read books?'

'Of course, they like reading despite their sanity.

Avadhesha was wonder struck.

In his country elderly people prefer to pray and perform religious rituals. They like to go on pilgrimage. They remain almost aliens to books.

Their faith in supernatural power is unique. They are almost wedded to the belief that someone is there carving their destinies.

'Time is essentially evil.' Avadhesha muttered the sentence into Martin's ear but he was busy driving. Avadhesha felt into a sort of reverie.

He started brooding over the past lives of the aged he met in the Nursing home.

Once they glowed like glow worms even in pitch darkness. They must have dreamt dreams, spoken soft words to their spouses and beloved with their fluttering hearts. But now for them everything is blackened like a dark.

It is opaque and impenetrable. Their emotional situations are tarnished.

'We are the hollow men . . . . We are the stuffed men, Between ideas and action their falls a shadow, Between conception and creation there falls a shadow.'

T.S Eliot's poetic lines crept into his sub-conscious like rays of the sun spreading radiance on the predicament of the old.

8

The pub, in the Rockdale was scattering symptoms of life in the most deserted hour of the night. An occasional horn of a vehicle created a stir and then subsided into silence. Of course the well dressed roads did not create any hindrance for anyone on the road.

It was a smooth sailing like a wave of the calm moving sea.

Apart from the illumination around the surroundings, the pub was pofously illuminated giving temptation to the passers-by.

There was a slow and small trickle of human beings at the entrance of the pub. Many shadowy figures were slipping away very quietly. Inside the pub occasional chats were audible and mild noise of wine and beer glasses arose as human lips touched them.

They did not gulp liquor. They sipped it gradually. A very small section of humanity was lost in the world of intoxication, an escape from realities of life.

Inside the pub in one of the corners sat small groups of chatters. They were chatting in different accents picking up vast raw threads of conversation.

They interwove all types of anecdotes impregnated with laughter, wit and professional advice. In the middle of the small assembly sat a bald-headed figure among them.

He looked like a sort of organizer of the group throwing pieces of advice to individuals according to their requirements and future needs.

At times he looked very intently at every face of the group. Avadhesha sat absolutely lost and mute in the group.

He felt dumb-founded as he was feeling completely ignored.

A sort of self-doubt arose in his mind creating a strange kind of void in his psyche.

He felt a kind of downward feelings in his mental crevices. He left his seat to occupy another one. His inner prompting was to launch an academic discussion but it did not get any support from any one of them.

Smith, a rather slightly bulky man, was busy talking to a Thai girl. His face looked fresh and comparatively younger. He spoke in almost Australian accent.

In fact he wanted to impact the Thai girl to a definite goal. His words directed towards her were tender and softer.

'Darling, would you mind another glass of beer?

They had already gulped in four to five glasses each.

The girl responded in a dim voice—'I don't mind. If you can . . .'

'Don't mind. I can do anything for you. Anything!'

The emphasis on 'Anything' was rather sinister and baffling.

Smith got up from his seat giving a soft push to his chair and slowly trotted towards the counter. He fetched two tumblers of beer and put them on the spot facing the girl.

'So you are an Iranian couple. You have come to Sydney. For what? In search of work? Am I correct?'

'Oh, yes,' the couple nodded their heads.

Michel was talking to each one of them as he was the main organizer. He leaned towards the Iranian girl.

'I'll do my best to get you a job. Don't you worry?'

Avadhesha sat quietly as no one talked to him.

He was given to some snatches of observing the entire sequence.

It was a kind of international community in the pub.

Quite a new experience and lot of girls to chat with.

A rare opportunity! A vital chance but he was forced to sit quiet.

Smith was observing the Thai girl as intoxication mounted her nerves.

Free beer to the girl. It was not motiveless.

Sinister designs . . .

Avadhesha shifted his seating and nestled in the vicinity of smith. He hardly showed any interest in Avadhesha's presence.

Avadhesha spoke to Smith rather hesitantly, 'Art-Gallery in NSW is superb. Quite a few of paintings are fantastic. I feel like writing about them.'

Smith hardly responded to Avadhesha's observation about his passion for paintings. His sole attention was on the seduction of the Thai girl. She too seemed to be involved in the situation.

Smith imparted a sly smile to her—'Move.'

'As you like!' She did not show any reluctance.

Avadhesha once more made an attempt to mention the Art-Gallery.

'Smith, an Art-Gallery is a reservoir of aesthetics.'

'Why not? Oh yes, why not?'

His response was highly casual and dismissing. To Smith that reference to Art-Gallery was just a dust-bin for him.

Michel was explicit in his inclination towards the Iranian girl.

'So Nassima, I suppose you are in search of some job.'

'We both are after jobs. We hold permanent visa to Australia.'

'That's fine.

'I will help you to the utmost. I have some resources and acquaintances. I'll connect them to you. You can be benefitted. I'm sure of that.'

For sometime quiet followed in the company. It was primarily prompted by intoxication riding the nerves of the group.

Avadhesha was feeling highly dejected as he could not converse his intellect to them.

Michel's neglect of him was deliberate as he could not tolerate the presence of a learned man.

Avadhesha was led into a contemplation.

Human nature is uniform and universal irrespective of caste, creed, religion, country or geographical conditions.

Michel's basic attempt was to assert his superiority. Suddenly an elderly lady participant started humming—

'Jingle bell, jingle bell all the way.'

Contours on her face and the way of her chanting the lines were quite amazing. A sentence of relaxation eased the company. But Smith seemed to be bent upon having the girl for the night.

There hung lust in his eyes. Smith was in constant contract with the girl during the entire sequence.

Avadhesha felt neglected and confused at the Australian accent of English. Though he was quite confident of his grasp over English yet here he found himself in a slightly ambiguous situation.

The night was advancing despite neon bulbs on the streets of Sydney. An occasional vehicle disturbed the tranquility of the road.

Scare pedestrians were visible in shaded spaces in front of shops. Avadhesha left the party in a huff.

It was not a very cordial parting. The Iranian girl was bent upon neglecting him.

He went out and found Smith looking for the Thai girl. He was in a state of grave intoxication. Avadhesha went near Smith to say good-buy when he whispered in his ears—'I think the girl has disappeared.'

'Which girl?' Avadhesha posed.

'The Thai girl, I was busy in drinking with. She promised to be with me in my car. I promised to drive her to her apartment.'

Avadhesha thought it wise not to comment on the situation but gave a halt to his hurrying footsteps to view the entire panorama.

Michel was still engaged with the Iranian couple. He was massively drunk and was trying to flirt with the Iranian girl who was experiencing a bit of embarrassment.

Suddenly an elderly, a middle aged Australian stood upon his feet and spoke in softer tones—

'Anyone for more drinks I'll love to serve. Yes, anyone?'

None of the party gave even a nod to the proposal. Avadhesha deemed it futile to linger on there. He was a bit fuming and fretting as he could not be an organic constituent of the party.

The Thai girl was there outside the pub and in a great affix whether to accompany Smith or not. Smith was intensely interested in having the girl with him. After all he had fed her beer and snacks to the brim.

Moreover he seemed to be in a mood to pay her some extra money also.

Avadhesha tried a bit to watch the entire spectacle. Smith coaxed the girl

'Why don't you come along? I'll drop you at your apartment.'

The girl prodded a few steps toward the car, hesitated a bit and then occupied the front seat in the vehicle.

Avadhesha's tipsy mind could visualize the sexual union of Smith and the Thai girl.

'No inhibitions, no taboos.'

Avadhesha muttered to himself—'What a freedom from social bondages and customs?'

He looked at neon bulbs brightening the road in totality. In his own country there are strong social fetters. These do not allow man to budge the beaten track.

Anything new is opposed or restricted. They invariably do not allow an individual or section of people to budge from their path. Anything new is resisted or criticized. A lot of social interference to freedom to curb intensive expression of one's basic nature.

Suddenly he was reminded of a Bulgarian who one day had fallen into a snappy conversation with him.

'But you don't give the impression of being an Indian. Your fair complexion and blue eyes betray some other nationality.'

'Oh, no, I am an Indian.'

Avadhesha was rather exceptionally emphatic about his identity.

'So you belong to the land of Kamasutra?'

The Bulgarian gave a chuckle to his face.

'By the way who was the author of the great classic? At the moment I am missing his name.'

Avadhesha furnished a prompt response to the query. 'I'm certain. It is Vatsyayna—a great Indian saint.'

'A saint?' The Bulgarian exposed his curiosity.

He continued his sense of amazement.

'A saint?

'Unbelievable! How can a saint write Kamasutra?'

'Why not?'

'It's just possible.'

'Our ancient saints were great scientists and observers of human life. They strived to study human life in totality.'

'Really?'

The Bulgarian once more came out with his curiosity.

The Bulgarian left his seat and made for the counter of the pub. He fetched a mug full of bubbling beer to the brim.

Politically he handed over the mug to Avadhesha. He smiled and spoke—'These are your wages for telling me the name of the author of Kamasutra.'

Avadhesha gave out a minor yell, 'oh . . . no . . .'

'What's wrong about it?'

'Let's sit and talk. These days I am reading a book—

'Dialogues with God.'

'It's rather nice of you to read and talk about books.'

Avadhesha lauded the Bulgarian.

'Reading . . . . provides me immense pleasure. It is a rewarding and a pure escape.'

'Of course . . . of course . . .'

Avadhesha was reminded of his native land. Majority hanker after gods and goddesses. Lectures full of wisdom, pieces of advice but hardly any implementation in practical life.

A big gulf between idea and action.

'Between idea and action there falls a shadow.' Avadhesha subconsciously was reminded of an utterance from T.S Eliot.

'So you are extremely fond of Kamasutra?'

Avadhesha bought a smile on his face.

'Yes, yes . . . it's a classic on sex. A monumental treatise.'

Avadhesha was highly impressed by the keen interest displayed by the Bulgarian.

'By the way are you interested in any nearby brothel?'

'Yes, why not?

Avadhesha muttered in chaos.

'Yes, there is one right on the opposite side of the road facing the pub.'

A brothel in the main stream of the bazaar!

'I can lead you to . . .'

'In my country they don't allow prostitution in any locality. It is considered a slur on the social set-up. They allow cheats, dishonest people, smugglers to live in social setup. But not a prostitute. She is a moral aberration, a pollutant of morals in the social milieu.'

'No such discrimination in Sydney. Prostitutes are a part of social establishment. No discrimination, no ostracization—no one looks down upon them. No respectable lady spits at her. It is simply a profession. It leads to survival, like other professions.'

'That's wonderful. Simply unbelievable. In my country prostitutes are confined to red light areas. They keep to themselves. They seldom mix up with common folks.

'Moralists dread the shadow of prostitutes. They are a slur, a stigma on our social make up and must be kept away.

'The same very moralists nestle near them in the night. They spend the most lusty moments in their company. They hug them, embrace and fuck them but are always under the umbrella of morals.

'In the morning they prepare faces to meet the faces. Of course a few of them feel pangs of conscience also. Their conscience makes them feel quietly and morally suffer for their pangs of morality.'

In Sydney even house-wives don't mind having a dig at morality. For some of them it is just O.K. Nothing unusual. Nothing abnormal. Nothing to give a prick to their moral set-up. Nothing extra ordinary.

The other day Avadhesha was sauntering along a beach. The sun stood in the sky like a watchman to entire humanity and other myriad of spices. All sorts of activities conglomerate to make a day. It takes diverse ways to complete its journey. It is a kind of movement that gives impetus to human life.

Each one of us has a feeling, he is living another day and doing something to give a purpose to his life and existence.

It's a kind of identity giving to its consciousness. Without identity a man's existence is drowned in nothingness. He starts doubting the very basic of his existence.

We see our reflections in our achievements accompanied by philosophical reflections. Avadhesha had a feeling that he was being neglected deliberately. Too much of individualism leads to a strange kind of mental loneliness and seclusion.

How to feel your existence?

Can you realize it in your own self?

No. You have people around you to make you realize the same.

Avadhesha was lost into a deep contemplation.

9

Human curiosity coupled with man's creativity has transformed the planet earth. But it is far from perfection. One thing or the other is always blighted. At times forces of nature become inhumanily disastrous and heap calamities on the planet.

But invariably beauty of nature also participates in human drama. It is curious unknown feature of life that is beyond our comprehension. Avadhesha stood on a lonely spot of the sea-beach and was lost in the remembrance of man's past on the earth.

The past can't be isolated from the present for it is everlasting, constant flow of human situations, experiences, adventures, events, ups and downs.

His eyes were focused on the vastness of the sea. He located some human figures emerging out of staircase descending to the downward direction. There he espied a park also receiving the last hues of the setting sun.

His eyes halting on the sun and then the spectacle of the young girl and the boy rolling in the waves of the sea. A strange apprehension appeared on his face. It was originated by the young couple involved in the sea-waves.

He espied the two coming in his direction. He feebly halted the young lady and apologetically asked her if she was not afraid of lusty sea-waves. There dawned a faint smile on the prominent contours of her face—'Oh, no, sir, thank you very much.'

'May I ask you a question?'

Avadhesha became aware of the absurdity of his question but could not restraint his tongue, 'Can you, gentle lady tell me the title and the author of the novel that contains graphic and vivid descriptions of the myriad aspects of the sea?'

The young lady in her swimming suit went into a mental search for two minutes and then spoke in full confidence, 'Hemming's The old man and the Sea.'

Avadhesha was quite pleased at the answer.

'Splendid?'

She thanked Avadhesha and followed in the direction of her lover. The setting sun was proceeding towards obscurity thereby giving existence to many man-made sources of light. He located a man coming in his direction. Avadhesha felt rather dazed at the appearance of a man whom he would be able to identify. But he was not sure of his conjecture.

His looked at him and the response was a bright smile. Avadhesha muttered to himself, 'He looks like an Indian. He cast an intense glance at him and enquired, 'From which country?'

'India.'

'Visiting or a citizen?'

'More than a citizen. My name is Shiv Kumar chaturvedi.'

'I see. I am glad to see you.'

'You too Indian?' Quipped the stranger.

'Oh, yes I'm visiting.'

'I see. Where do you live?

'With my son at Kogarah. And what about you?'

'I live at Paramata.'

Chaturvedi's reply was quick. 'I have no family. I live alone.'

Avadhesha experienced a bit of dismay and further enquired, 'I see. By the way how come you live alone? And where is your family?'

'Somewhere in India. I don't know the extract city or town.'

Avadhesha felt that mystery was depeening.

'Come along with me. Mine is a harrowing tale to disclose. Simply aweful harrowing and awe inspiring.'

'I can't restrain my curiosity,' Avadhesha uttered in vast chaos.

He felt a bit of tremble in his body. There was a shaky strain in his voice as he had developed misgivings for the man. He might be a criminal or a drug-addict. It was rather difficult to discern.

Avadhesha looked at chaturvedi. He had slowed down his walking. Time and again, Avadhesha was feeling insecure.

Sea-waves were restless in hitting the precincts of the enclosed area.

Avadhesha asked him furtively, 'Have you lost something at the spot where stairs are situated?'

'Yes, my youth, my family, my everything'.

Avadhesha came out with fear and anxiety. He was sensitively curious of the distant boats and the surface of the vast ocean.

'Do you locate that beautified dungeon located near the stair-case?' Chaturvedi turned, stopped and raised his pointing figure towards that location.

'Dungeon?' Avadhesha looked at him with a lot of amazement.

'Yes, a dungeon. I was made a captive there and forced to live in *Kala Pani*—a sort of life-long punishment'.

'By whom?'

'The Britishers, yes, the Britishers. I was a *satyagrahy* in the full support of Gandhi.'

Avadhesha felt the shock of his life and sympathy for Chaturvedi. He became actuely aware of the forces of malevolent fate. 'We were rather starved of food and basic amenities of life. The only remanant of those days is the wild sea and no other human habilitation. '*Kala-Pani* do you know and understand this Hindi word? It smacks of something sinister and harrowing.'

Avadhesha's eyes were set and he stretched his imagination to the plagued periods of British history. 'Are you the lone example of this kind of unhappy situation in this area?'

'Oh, no, no, you seem to be ignorant of India's struggle for freedom from the yoke of the Britishers.

'How come?' Avadhesha registered a set-back to his ego.

He was dismayed at his own ignorance.

His finger moved in a zig-zag manner to betray his mental restlessness.

He looked at Shiv Kumar with some hidden awe. His face carried a faint colour of being snubbed.

'The British empire, you know was sprawling over many areas of the world. All types of prisoners including the aboriginals of this country were forced to live in this cell. They wee subjected to all types of atrocities. Each day brought new spectacles of horrors and deaths. The dead bodies were offered to sea-crevices to have a repast.

Avadhesha's mental and physical structure was in the grip of fear and dread. Time and again, he cast a glance at the direction of the down-stairs and the sea howling steadily.

'What for do you visit this area? Your name sir?. Shiv Kumar.'

'I come here to recollect dark days of my youth'.

'To what advantage sir?' Avadhesha displayed his curiosity with a lot of concern for Shiv Kumar.

'I do not exactly understand the so-called advantage, but I can't exactly express myself. In a way it gives significance to my existence in the world. I lived for the sake of my motherland and followed the foot-steps of Gandhi, a great man of the present times. No less satisfying one learns from sufferings.

'True-true,' Avadhesha almost touched Shiv Kumar's feet.

'Oh, no, no, please. No dearth of great men in this world. Some people achieve rare things in this world. My hats off to them.'

Shiv Kumar extracted his diary from his pocket and jotted down Avadhesha's whereabouts and telephone number. Avadhesha followed the same ritual with the help of his mobile. The sun, meanwhile had taken massive strides into the downward deep into the sea.

Shiv Kumar looked at Avadhesha and indicated his wish to depart.

'I am immensely glad to see you. Sheer coincidence. 'Coincidences play a vital role in human situations.

'Oh, yes, of course. In life everything is not rational and self-explanatory. The blue from the above conjures many things and imparts to us a strange mystery of the hidden and the unexpected.'

Avadhesha nodded a massive acceptance of Shiv Kumar's philosophical assertion.

Shiv Kumar while bidding farewell to Avadhesha drew his attention in serious tones, 'I believe you have come to visit Sydney. From your looks you seem to be inquisitive rather good. It is a beautiful city of myriad aspects. It is a multicultural city granting existence to people from all over the world. They are allowed to follow their own cultures, ways of life and rituals but live in strict accordance with the laws of the country. Fantastic and wonderful. After all human heart and human psyche are the same, only it manifests in different dresses, languages and expressions.'

Shiv Kumar approved of Avadhesha's observations on human life.

Avadhesha was left lonely on the sea-beach. He looked at sea-waves gaining speed and strength. He started musing over man's mortality and Nature's eternity. Words worth, the great poet of nature, sang—'its beauty is dead but nature is alive and kicking. And it is ever lasting. Its rhythm is ever-lasting and ever mysterious.'

He started walking away from the sea-shore towards human-habitation. More people, more vehicles and more hustle and bustle signifying the existence of human activities.

'Hello, how are you? What are you doing here at this hour?'

Avadhesha concentrated on the figure approaching him with big strides.

'Hello, how are you? Surprised to see you here! How come you are here? What for?' Avadhesha came across a migrant from Pakistan.

'I'm glad to see you. Rather very glad to see you. You, looking down? What for? Let's go for a glass of beer.'

Rahim readily accepted the invitation. His spirits seemed buoyed to a small extent. 'with great pleasure. Let us sit down'.

'I have a sad tale to narrate.'

'Why, What happened?'

'Let us first sit down,' Rahim was reluctant to talk to him.

The pub was sufficiently illuminated and full of soothing music. The pub accommodated many men and women creating a cosmopolitan atmosphere. At the counter stood two beautiful girls selling wares.

Avadhesha neared the counter and ordered two glasses of beer and fetched them on the table in front of Rahim. Rahim slowly sipped the contents of the glass and explained to Avadhesha his cause of not attending church for sometime. 'I'm, facing a problem,' he muttered feebly to Avadhesha.

'What sort of problem?' Avadhesha betrayed his curiosity. He had been meeting Rahim in church for quite sometime and exchanging their conversations in vernacular. To talk in their native language was a sort of pleasure to them. They often exchanged views on Indo-Pak relationship and many other problems facing their countries. The glasses were deprived of their contents and the two were in a heightened moral.

'Why, what's wrong with you?'

Avadhesha attempted to draw Rahim's attention diverted on the breasts of a woman seated on the next sofa. Her breasts were oozing out of their allotted area and gave sensation to the on-looker.

'Rahim, where have you lost yourself?'

'I'm sorry, very sorry. I felt diverted'.

'Oh! none of your fault. It's natural with us.' A faint smile sat on Avadhesha face.

'My two children—'

Rahim's face was beclouded with sorrow.

'What happened to your children?'

'They have been taken away by some authorities of Australian govt.'

Avadhesha's lips were suspended in bafflement.

'To what fault? The other day I came across you, your wife and all your children. Kids were well-seated in a pram and the grown-ups were on foot'. Avadhesha tried to remind him of their abrupt meeting across the princess high way. 'All of you seemed to be quite well.'

'No doubt. Whatever you are saying to absolutely correct, Only a fortnight before.' Rahim's face looked dismayed and his eyes got focused on vacancy. Suddenly he picked up his courage and declared, 'I have filed a suit in the court against the govt. It's violation of parental feelings'

'How come?' Avadhesha was rather taken aback

'They have no right to deprive me of my children. How can they live without parents? It is true my children can't talk English. How can they be blamed for this? They are brought up where the first language is not English but Urdu. At home we converse in Urdu'.

'That's absolutely correct' Avadhesha looked at Rahim in full support of his point of view.

'We can't find fault. Absolutely innocent and ignorant. It is true we are asylum seekers but there are laws to govern us too.'

Rahim was feeling extremely dejected and revolted against the existing situation not created by his efforts to lead a beautiful life in Sydney. He gulped another glass of beer to smoothe his smoldering nerves.

Rahim was sympathetic and trying to reach some common conclusions for mankind. He mused that problems are common to all people all over the world. You may belong to any country, sorrows and joys are a common inheritance of humanity. These are unescapable because these are a part of man's existence on the earth. Rahim too was in a paltry and shaky stake of mind following a domestic situation.

He touched his balding head and uttered in utter dejection—'Allah!' I seek protection in you. You are the only shelter I can look forward. You are the only saviour of me to whom I can look to in my extreme distress.'

Tears were visible in Rahim's eyes. 'Man's existence on the planet earth a curious mixture of joys and sorrows. We just can't escape them. They are inevitable but nothing lasts longer.' Rahim chuckled to himself.

Avadhesha touched Rahim's hand and patted it in the manner of consolation. He too felt much grief for Rahim's children. Only parents and children feel the pangs of separation. Rahim, under the spell of intoxication was wild with ejaculation of invectives. His anger and desperation were quite audible to Avadhesha. He addressed himself as well as Avadhesha—'I have already filed a legal suit against the government claiming damages for my children, for the time being there seems to be no way out of this tanglement.'

Both walked out of the pub having given last finishing touches to their glasses. They walked a few paces in union and separated from each other after exchanging proper salutations.

Avadhesha was in a mood of great bewilderment and was jumpy in his nerves. He muttered to himself—'Human sorrow is common to people at large Countries, languages and places do not matter. Similarly natural calamities are a common inheritance to man irrespective of country, caste and creed. In a way Nature's ways are impartial to all species on the planet, earth. She does not discriminate. It is equanimous to man at large.'

Suddenly Avadhesha wsa reminded that it was Sunday. He must visit the temple of Lord Krishna in North Sydney. Lord Krishna is bound to prove a source of consolation to him. He must give some relief to his distraught nerves. He headed towards the nearby station to board a train bound for North Sydney. After the lapse of an hour he entered the premises of the temple. It was a cloudy night. Clouds had swung in without issuing any warning. Darkness was hardly visible due to sources of illumination hung on poles.

He entered the portals of the temple. A crowd of devotees to Lord Krishna was lost in harmonious chant in praise of Lord Krishna. He headed straight towards the inner sanctum of Lord Krishna and paid him all the reverence at his disposal. He was feeling at home in the temple. Devotees were dancing, enacting, bowing with drum-beat accompanying hymns and chanting of *Hare Krishna-Hare Rama*. It was a vibrant environment of melodious harmony pervading the entire community. Avadhesha was simply wonder struck at the spectacle in the temple. He experienced an emotional and spiritual elevation and once more stepped towards Lord Krishna and bowed before him for several moments. Lord Krishna's gracious presence in Sydney speaks of his omni-presence in the entire cosmos.

All kinds of rituals were being observed in the portals of the temple. It was Avadhesha's maiden visit to this holy place. He stepped out and located a shop right in the centre of the temple selling all sorts of wares relating to Lord Krishna. Outside the temple a lot many devotees were busy eating *Prasad*. They sat in groups and enjoyed delicacies being served by volunteers at the counter. It was a very engrossing sight. He observed the prominent contours of the temple and felt a throb of ecstasy. But he did not come across a single known face to him. He spoke to himself—'It takes time to cultivate acquaintance.' Meanwhile he came upon a queer old man in the company of his son. They had cornered themselves and seemed to be in a state of quarrelsome dialogue. The old man was expressing his mental dejection and was speaking to his son in anger. Fortunately no one was aware that transpined between the father and the son. Avadhesha drew himself near them and listened to their slightly high-pitched conversation.

'Why did you bring me here?' The old man spoke in vernacular.

'Father, you should be glad to be in Lord Krishna's presence, you must feel the omni-presence of Lord Krishna.' The son attempted to gladden his father.

'Of course, that I do I really feel the manifestation of Lord Krishna every where. 'But . . . ?' the old man was in a mood of dejection.

'But what . . . ? The son widened his brows in curiosity.

'But the indecent behaviour of that young Englishmen.

One of the *gopies* was in the arms of the youngman, Shame, shame. *Gopies* whether English or Indian belong to Lord Krishna only. Only god is allowed to have music and dancing with *gopies*.'

'Ture, true, absolutely true, absolutely true.' The son tried his best to give mental ease to his old father.

'Father, everything is far from perfection. All types of human situations arise. Different people have divergent thoughts and actions. And each one of us has some short-comings.'

The old man from India seemed to be in mental dejection at this minor moral aberration of the english youngman.

The son addressed his father calmly, 'Father, let's go. It is growing late. I have to attend my office in the morning'.

After their departure, Avadhesha was feeling quite amused at the situation. If one sticks to one's beliefs, it is not possible to dodge him from that mental situation.

He entered the main portals of the temple where Lord Krishna's praise was being chanted in a loud unison. It was like a crescendo falling and rising in melodious voice. There was a constant inflow of devotees of all ages and of different nationalities. To Avadhesha it was a matter of great gratification to watch this conglomeration. It was nothing less than ecstasy to hear Lord Krishna's praise through singing and chanting. It was a kind of prayer to Lord Krishna for salvation and freedom from sins.

10

Glimmsing landscape of sky-scapers of Sydney, after the dawn, had advanced a bit. The arrival of the morning was usual but very fast and was involved in a natural brisk pace. Everyone seemed to be in a hurry. Well-dressed girls, women and decorated dolls were always lost in themselves. There seemed to be a universal hurry to reach the place of their work. Their foot steps were caught in a kind of urgency. Quick steps, hardly aware of passers-by and rushing vehicles at fast pace. The sole agenda was mechanical and constant without any respite or diversion. It was a constant flow of humanity without any break or a chance to glimpse the attractive sky-scapers formed of different presences in the sky.

Avadhesha was at the moment on a paved path sauntering at this duration to capture the crescendo of human life. The sun was already declining with its full brightness paving its way to the zenith in the sky. He felt sensitively lonely in the constant flow of humanity. But the flow of humanity was isolated in embryonic cells. On the contrary Avadhesha was pining for a real human situation. His wish was materialized where a sharp feminine giggle pierced his ears. He turned back to locate a young girl in the lap of a boy. He lusty, naked legs and thoughts were well-lapped in his embrace. The girl was full of bovine laughter and was in the grip of a tricky situation. Its nothing less than thrilling and he leaned forward to kiss her eyes. 'How lusty and attractive are your legs! Provocative sexually and highly inflammable.'

'Thanks a lot.' The girl offered an intimate hug to the boy triggering her in his lap.

Avadhesha had a sneaky sight of human sepctacle presented to him. He felt baffled to see that the surroundings of the spectacle remained neutral to the provocative sight. Avadhesha felt tickled and amused at the scene. It could not be possible in his country. It would attract a lot of crowd and might lead to a severe thrashing of the hero and the heroine for this little enactment.

It was bound to find a mention in one of the local newspapers of the country and none local speaker would comment upon the falling standards of morality.

Avadhesha is suddenly reminded of a native of Sydney whom he finds sitting on a bench almost everyday. The bench is fixed and so is the man. To him he gives the impression of lost soul drowned in the layers of his sub-conscious. Many a time Avadhesha sits by him, tries to tickle him and they remain communicative to each other. 'Are you alone in the city? No wife? No son? No daughter?'

He emits a brief giggle and starts muttering something really inaudible. His face is contracted like a frightened pigeon. His creeping voice gives out a dim audibility. One day Avadhesha finds him smoking. He seems to be in a different mood. The smoke from his cigarette is creating a small area of pollution. He relaxes his nerves. Avadhesha is already seated by his side on the bench. The flow of humanity in the market is constant. Avadhesha is baffled to observe that not a single human being in the market looks at them. They don't tarry even a bit. Every walker or customer is confined to his own existence. He is reminded of T.S. Eliot's poetic line. 'I had not thought Death had undone so many.'

Avadhesha makes several attempts of talking to him but his murmuring is beyond his comprehension 'what's your name?

'Henry!' Heal more blurts out.

'Where do you live?'

He murmurs the name of a colony beyond Avadhesha's understanding.

'Got any wife, son or daughter?'

'My wife died ten years ago. No son. No daughter. I live alone. It's a place away. Yes . . . . away.'

'Away means? Avadhesha would understand the physical dimensions of the word 'away'. Henry started peeping into his bag. Avadhesha was also tempted to cast a sly glance into Henry's bag. There were tablets, cigarettes, packets and a few more articles wrapped in a piece of cloth. Henry directed his stare at Avadhesha for several seconds and then suddenly enquired of him's. 'Do you smoke?'

Avadhesha was in a dilemma. He nodded his head feebly in a kind of acceptance. He looked at Henry's face. Contours on his face were a bit contracted. His half-opened lips were waiting a response to his query.

'Yes, at times I smoke but very casually. A cigarette or two per week.

He offered a cigarette to Avadhesha and lighted it too.

'How do you spend your day?' Avadhesha picked a question for Henry.

'You see, you see. I come here in the market—say about ten o' clock. I sit through the day.'

'Does some one talk to you? Any one to share what passes in your mind?'

He was puzzled at this question.

'Share? What? Oh . . . no . . . not much passes in my mind. I'm used to it.'

Avadhesha was baffled at the loneliness of this man.

No one to talk to him at home. All alone in the market despite a massive flow of vehicles and humanity. A tide of disciplined chaos in the market.

'Any neighbour around where you live?'

It was a bit difficult to understand Avadhesha's Indian accent of English. It was a stunted communication between the two.

'I have neighbours. No talk to me.' He gradually understood Avadhesha's question, puff of the cigarette and deposited the butt in the nearby bin. He sits in his dense isolation. No one shares his mind. Avadhesha lets himself fall into a strain of abstract philosophical speculation.

It is not the predicament of the modern man? Cut off, dead confinement to an unknown, unrealized self. In India people are highly communicative. They talk on diverse random topics and issues not directly related to them. Talking or sharing is a pleasure to them. Gradually they are also being enveloped in morbid self-centrality but still a lot is left which is human and related. Avadhesha was sad at Henry's pligat. He must give him company for some time and be in his vicinity for sometime in order to share the weight of sub-conscious mind.

Henry looked at him with a baffled curiosity. He was amazed at the idea of a human being offering to sit with him and talk to him.

He kept on focusing his glance at him and whispering 'what job were you in as a young man?'

Avadhesha was not interested in making the communication more formal.

'Builder' there was an expression of pride on his face.

'Builder?' Avadhesha gave another intense glance to him. A builder is very important man in Indian social set-up. He is supposed to be very rich, well connected and resourceful.

'You, a builder? How many buildings did you bring in existence?'

'Many . . . ?

But he did not give the impression of being a builder. May be his advancing age and unfortunate circumstances brought him to this relegated stature.

'You must have old connections as a builder. You must have earned a lot of wealth and a wonderful house to live in.'

It took him some time to interpret what Avadhesha spoke to him.

'No, no . . . ,' he pretented vehemently.

'I worked as a builder . . .'

Avadhesha took some time to understand Henry's talk about his job. He made it a point to sit with him almost everyday. At times they would pick up hazy conversation.

One day Henry picked up a very personal issue.

'You see, I married two women as a young man. My first wife met with an accident. With my second wife I could not carry on for long. It resulted in divorce. She took away the son born to us. I wanted to keep the child but the court did not permit.'

Avadhesha looked at his face and tried to console him and tried to be sympathetic to him.

Suddenly clouds approached in the sky imparting a cold tinge to the weather. Henry started building his bits.

'See you later on'. He left Avadhesha in a jiffy after an exchange of formal salutations. Henry's chapter of youth was left unfinished to Avadhesha. Avadhesha himself was keen to have conversation. He craved for company that could listen to his feelings.

For many days Henry was not seen on the bench.

Avadhesha was almost confused. He always located Henry on the bench on his way to the library.

Apart from the members of our family, we feel the necessity of talking to people. Communication with a fellow being is of utmost importance, otherwise we are left alone with our brain cells to weave a net work of internecine conflicts. It may lead to a sort of tension. Avadhesha always took care to exchange solutions and conversation with the women at the library counter. It imparted a kind of sense of having some human touch.

At times he deliberately would walk into a shop and start making all sorts of enquiries. That would give some sort of mental relief to him. In the library, visitors maintained a kind of monolithic silence. What information could he elicit about Henry? Strange! no one knows anything about him.

Avadhesha felt wonder-struck.

In his own country people keep full information about others they mentally step into many house-holds for positive or negative pleasure. At least a sense of concern is there. They nourish a kind of curiosity. Here they have no interest in other human beings. Their primary concern is only themselves. On the road they walk like robots as if their existence is confined only within the physical dimensions of their existence. Primal human concerns are thrown to dogs. Their basic attitude to life is that of a shopkeeper culminating in 'Thank you very much.'

One afternoon Avadhesha was glad to locate Henry on the bench. He rushed towards him on the bench. 'You were not around for many days. Strange, everything O.K?'

'I was taken ill. No one to take care of me.'

Avadhesha was full of pity for him.

'You could ring me up.' Avadhesha expressed his sympathy for him.

These was a brief sardonic smile on Henry's face. 'How could I ring you up? No telephone number with me. Moreover I was bed-ridden.'

Henry's face was pale and an evidence to his helplessness. He twitched his lips and gazed at Avadhesha. Avadhesha fell into a kind of apprehension for him. Avadhesha noticed an evil change in Henry. He seemed to be on the verge of a collapse. He registered a head-long trembling of his lips. His breathing gradually was collapsing into an effort. What could Avadhesha do? He did not know how to manage the situation. He looked at many pedestrians but they did not respond. He felt aghast at the lack of human concern. He rushed inside a chemist stop. The chemist did not come out but was kind enough to give a ring at the hospital. A ring at hospital in his country may or may not get any response. But here he was surprised to see an ambulance arriving at the spot in no time. It was well-equipped. By that time Henry lay unconscious on the bench. No one stopped to look at the unconscious patient. No crowds. No passive spectators of his own native land. The doctors on the ambulance got down and started examining the patient. They injected some medicines in the patient and waited for a reaction. After half an hour Henry fettered his eyelids and showed feeble symptoms of consciousness. Avadhesha heaved a sigh of relief. Henry was to be transported to hospital in the ambulance. Avadhesha was a little scared when he spoke to the doctor. 'How is Henry? Beyond danger?'

The doctor looked at him rather curiously.

'You know him? Is he related to you? In the hospital we have to do some proper proceedings in Henry's situation.'

'No, no . . . I am his co-bencher.'

'What do you mean?' The doctor inquired of Avadhesha with visible suspense on his face.

'I often talk to him.'

'What for?'

'To relieve him of his loneliness. I just feel like conversing with him.'

'Now what do you want me to do?' The doctor made an enquiry.

'I want to know the location and address of the hospital.'

'St. Geoge hospital is situated at Kograli. You come at the reception and then make enquiries. Timings for visiting a patient are fixed. Come between four to six in the evening.'

Henry was put in the ambulance and taken away to hospital. Avadhesha seated himself on the bench and was lost into all types of speculations. Not a single passer-by had stopped near Henry. What human apathy? Simply astonishing. What a neglect of human connections? But the ambulance had arrived very quickly and promptly. Henry was given a quick and on the spot treatment.

Avadhesha thinks of crowds that collect around such incidents and accidents in India. But they keep away from the victim. They fear a police action against them also. They have their own apprehensions regarding such situations. In small towns it is quite difficult to have on the spot treatment. But sometimes victims or patients are transported to hospitals by unknown people. But invariably an accident is a matter of spectacle. Morbid ideas entered Avadhesha's mind. At least Henry will be able to talk to nurses, doctors and other members of the hospital. At least his monolithic loneliness would disappear.

Henry will be surrounded by more human activities.

Scattered clouds in the sky were going astray without any specific direction.

The setting sun was partially peeping the holes created by the peculiar situation of the sky space. Avadhesha stood alone on the thresh hold of his house looking depressed and in deep contemplation where to go to cheer up, yes—to R.S.L. Club. But whenever he goes there, he comes out chatless.

He hardly gets any emotional boost up. Of course a change in place changes one's mental situation also.

Avadhesha felt an on-rusa of flash and visualized Henry in hospital. 'Why not to go and make enquiries about Henry's recovery? Yes, he must go. That would add a lot of cheer to Henry's mental make up and a boost to his own mental blockage.' He dressed himself and came down the lift and boarded a bus to St. George Hospital.

Boarding a bus in India? A shudder swept through his body. Enormous crowds, sometimes heading towards a stampede.

He seated himself comfortably in the bus and alighted comfortably in front of St. George Hospital. He briefly walked towards the information desk. The premises looks quite conducive to visitors. These are indicators and sufficient number of signs for the visitor to locate patients. Yes, Henry was there looking not all trodden and sullen. He seemed to have picked up his spirits and not to be in a mood of utter relaxation.

'Hello, Henry I'm really delighted to see you. You are O.K.? you look more relaxed and expressive'

Henry strained his eyes to give full recognition to Avadhesha's voice and facial expressions. He made a humble gesture for him to be comfortably seated on a chair near Henry's bed. The room had basic medical equipment to make him comfortable.

'How do you feel here? Must be more comfortable than the bench in Rockdale?'

'What do you say? I'm used to sitting there. I don't feel that lonely as you seem to think. I miss something, my friends.'

Avadhesha was almost dumb founded at the mention of the word 'friends.'

He repeated rather mechanically.

'Friends!

'Oh . . . Pigeons.'

'Yes, yes do you see them enjoying my feed to them? Do n't you see flutter in their feathers? I never feel lonely in a way. I am visited by them everyday. I watch their manifold activities.'

'Do you feel related with them?'

'Of course, of course.'

There was visible gladness on Henry's face. He seemed to be over joyed at the prospect of meeting them again.

Avadhesha shook hands with Henry and walked out of the room not much dissatisfied.

'But we can relate ourselves to any animate or inanimate object. With birds, with animals to any species created by God.'

On his way back home in the train, Avadhesha grew quite contemplative. He remembered Mathew Arnold's line—'We millions live alone.'

Avadhesha's conjecture was almost correct. Except him no one else had paid visit to him. He felt moved at Henry's plight. Without family a man is like the first man on the planet. He feels unrelated and deracinated.

Avadhesha's conjecture was correct that the city has many loners. But what's the origin of this seclusion? Man by instinct is a social animal. The chief blame goes to the growth of a materialistic and self-centered social set-up. Everyone to himself. Our planet has myriad blessings and draw-backs, an outcome of natural causes. Man of to-day has multiplied his misfortunes because of his self centrality. He must revisit Henry at least after a week.

He hails from a different social set-up. At least this kind of segregation is not there in his native land. There they keep up negative or positive relationship. This kind of neutrality is not there. They are related through religious, customs and festivals. This gregarious instinct gives to them a kind of psychological shelter and a sense of belonging. Eugene O Neill's play—'The Hairy Ape' swam into his memory. The protagonist desperately searches for a sense of belonging and unfortunately, he is unable to find one. This leads him to physical and psychological extinction.

Avadhesha once more paid a visit to the hospital premises to inquire about Henry.

The setting sun was peeping through painted window-panes and starting creeks of the hospital. A cold shivering day ending with bright sunshine He was reminded of T.S. Eliot's poetic utterance—'Winter evening settles down with smell of steaky passage ways.

Six O' clock.

Burnt out ends of smoky day, the little cab steams and stamps.

And then lightening of lamps.'

Avadhesha felt a kind of shiver pass through the structure of his body. He remembered Whitman's lines implying.

'If you want to talk to a stranger. Why not to talk to him?'

He found himself in the lift in the company of two beautiful girls. What charming faces to look at? He was eager to talk to them but wouldn't say 'hello' to them checked from within by a kind of hesitation.

He knocked at Henry's room but drew a blank. There was no one to respond. He gave a slight push to the door and peeped into it to find berefit of Henry. Its interior was blank but not awesome. He turned back and found a nurse facing him. Curiosity was writ large on his face as the sister kept on walking around. 'I came to see Henry, patient in this room.'

He pointed with his finger the half-open door. A kind of curious expression sat on his face.

'Henry . . . o, yes he is transported to a brothel, the nurse delivered a piece of information without any moral hassles. Avadhesha received an electric shock at this disclosure of the nurse. He was staring at the lady all surprised.

'That's the prerogative of patients. We don't allow them to starve sexually. Expenses of the brothel are borne by the patient. Ambulance service is free.' The sister slipped away leaving Avadhesha in the clutches of amazement. He almost rolled down on a nearby bench almost in a state of semi-consciousness. Henry, the patient visiting a brothel? Almost a shell shock to him.

The fabric and forts of morality began to crumble like the bricks of a decaying structure. All his concepts of morality were scattered to dilapidated ruins.

He fumbled to himself—'Here they recognize the sanctity and individuality of basic instincts. Suppression leads to perversion.'

Moreover the sister gave to him Henry's whereabouts without any self-consciousness or blushing. Meanwhile he thought with the proceedings of a book-chat to which he is a regular participant. An old lady named Kathy was reading records of the main events of her life. She had penned down almost everything of her that had occurred in life time. A few photographs of her youth were also displayed among the audience present in the room.

It does not allow anything except human soul which also is beclouded in a chain of uncertainties. But death is a reality that no one can obliterate. In Avadhesha's vicinity sat a slightly well-built lady and the remanasits of her prime youth. There appeared a sudden, abrupt gleam on her face born out of a spontaneous mischief when she raised a query—'Kathy, let me know if condoms were used when you were young.'

Kathy acquired a composure on her old, decaying face and the question remained unanswered. But the lady repeated her question and burst into a big laughter. The question died its own death.

Avadhesha thought no moral hassles, no conflict and absolutely no moral conscience. It was as plain and usual as drinking a glass of water. In his country, he could not conceive of such naked remarks in the contexts of sex. Yes, cultures are diverse. Is it not unique and curious to see our basic, universal instincts getting social channels in diverse ways? And at times conflicts arise merely manifest themselves in divergent ways because due to the social, climatic situations, religious rituals and individual and collective consciousness of a nation or a community. There arose a small creak and then went in and closed it. Avadhesha was glad that Henry was back from the brothel and Avadhesha was in a mood to tease him. He followed him inside the room and faced Henry with a broad smile on his face. A beaming smile on his face indicated that something wonderful had been accomplished by him. He looked at Avadhesha rather curiosly.

'Where have you been Henry?

'To-day I'm very happy and feeling much relaxed.'

A sardonic smile spread on his face. Avadhesha smiled back because he knew the back-ground of the entire episode.

'How come you are feeling relieved?'

'Oh! The girl was smart and co-operative. It was accomplished with the doctor's consent. I had to buy the girl.'

He narrated the entire episode as if he had been on some pilgrimage.

Avadhesha could not believe that a person could be that explicit about the psychological aspect of sex. He thought about the general outlook of people to sex. Invariably they indulge in these activities secretly. They would try to hide such incidents to every extent. They would like all these activities. To themselves polygamy is a sort of sin in his country. For a married man it is extra-ordinarily prohibited, otherwise he opens the gates of hell for himself. People in his own land are quite conservative and don't allow such things to happen.

It was 7 O'clock in the evening. Avadhesha took leave of Henry. Before his departure Henry informed him that he will be discharged within a week and then he will report back to his bench. He was feeling rather excited at his prospect of going back to his area created by his consciousness. He would meet a group of pigeons and take delight in meeting and feeding them. Despite enjoying the company and presence of his old friends. Avadhesha shook hands with him and wished him good luck at his departure from the room.

The evening was placid, far flung and global at least in this region of the earth. The hospital lights were hit and an ambience of illumination existed in the hospital and without also.

Avadhesha took his way to the lift and pressed the button for its operation.

Meanwhile a girl stepped near the lift. She seemed to be twenty five years old. Her face looked soft and slightly bright. A sort of dimness sat on her body. She kept on staring at Avadhesha without a blink in her eyes. Avadhesha was slightly puzzled because usually girls did not look at him. Except Irene no other girl gave him any emotional support. And now Irene too had withdrawn. He was left lingering in an emotional void of great magnitude. At times he fluttered his wings to trace a kind of emotional shelter but all his attempts came to nothing.

He started back at the girl with a slow drawl, 'hello,'

The girl responded with a broad smile.

By that time the lift had become visible and both entered the lift. At the moment they were the sole occupants of the lift and Avadhesha did not receive the intensity of the stare of the girl. The lift touched the ground floor and the two came out of it. Contrary to Avadhesha's expectations, the girl did not rush away.

Avadhesha advanced a few feet towards her and feebly enquired of her, 'would you like to spend some time in my company? Let's have a small chat.'

'Why not? Why not?'

The girl was rather emphatic.

There lay a bench adjoining the lawn. It was an inviting place to sit, chat and relax.

'What's your name? may I ask you?'

'Of Course, of Course. Na-Dine'.

Avadhesha looked at her in a kind of bewilderment.

She brought a smile on her face, 'Italian name?'

'You from Italy?'

'Yes, I was born there. My father is an Italian and mother Australian.'

'Cross-breed?'

She felt a bit up-set

'Oh, no, I am cosmopolitan.'

'That's wonderful.'

'In which subrub you live?'

'Brighten.'

'How lucky!'

"How?'

'You, almost live in the vicinity of the sea?'

'That's correct, I always feel the immensity of the sea. Awe inspiring. A potent source of awe and vastness. Whenever I look at it, I imagine the endless tiny specks of consciousness.

'How candid and expressive?'

Avadhesha nestled a bit near this recent acquaintance casting a penetrating glance at her. A curious combination of brightness and something ebbing out. He felt a sort of pity for her. It didn't look common but carried a faint impression of mental sickness.

The evening had almost vanished into the remote corners of the sky.

'May I know the cause of your sickness? You seem to be off your spirits.'

'Yes, I at times don't feel normal. I feel either escastic or depressed. I feel either elevated or thrown into a vast ditch.'

'Strange!' Avadhesha uttered the word with a lot of restrain.

'How did you infect this malady?'

'What do you imply?

Avadhesha's voice was rather husky.

'My father was a victim of this disease. He is an Italian and lives away from the family. I seldom meet him.'

She brought a faint smile on her face.

The smiling contours of her face were still grief stricken. But were obvious enough to attract the attention of a casual spectator. She glanced at Avadhesha rather peevishly on the same bench perched in the grassy lawn of the hospital. The number of freanenters in the hospital was dwindling because of the hours that left patients without visitors.

'How come? Are you an author?'

'Yes, in a way. But I maintain writing as a hobby. A sort of relief form conscious and subconscious areas of mind.'

'Tensions?'

Na-Dine raised her eye-lids in an impatient enquiry.

'Yes, writing is an excellent art of unburdening our sub-conscious—a reservoir of our suppressed regressions and experiences. It is like a vast reservoir without any physical dimensions. It's rather impossible to fathom its dimensions in physical terms. It is an ever-expanding reservoir to feelings, notions, basic tendencies and appetencies.'

'Quite psychological, analytical' she spoke in her brimming tempo.

'But creativity is not just sub-conscious but is craft also promoted by emotive factors. It is a kind of sensitive response to beauty and ugliness. It is an author's imaginative propensity.'

'Beautiful, indeed.' She clapped her small palms in a kind of unison. She looked at Avadhesha with a pathetic expression in her benign and hurt eyes. It was the dawn of self pity and helplessness out of which there seemed to be no escape.

'How old are you?'

'About 45.'

'But you look a teen.'

Her spirits flared up at the compliment.

'What about your mother?'

'She lives her own from me and my father. But my contacts with my mother are O.K. We are on telephone for eachother once a day. But I don't want to lose my independence at all.

'That's amazing.'

'How amazing?'

There was a mixed expression on her face. It was neither annoying nor pleasing. Avadhesha expressed himself rather reluctantly—'A diseased daughter living away from her mother? How do you sustain yourself?'

'Oh . . . . how many questions I am supposed to answer? How many?'

She emitted a giggle of small frequency and pitch.

'I have my fixed clients.'

The word client suggested something immoral to Avadhesha. He, unconsciously, was led into suspicion regarding the moral standards of Na-Dine.

She is brutally frank.

'I can't understand your abnormal quiet.'

'I oh! I suppose you are tricked into the word 'client.'

'How do you surmise?'

'I have a way to understand people. Sixth sense.'

Avadhesha burst into a small giggle.

'Why do you laugh. Indians have a way of thinking. I have come across many.'

Avadhesha felt a bit offended.

'Please elaborate your sentence and the intention of the sentence.'

'Indians sometimes walk into wrong lanes. They more than often walk into morality related contexts and start doubting everything.'

'It is very clever of you to talk like this. Every nation has some characteristics.'

'Yes, that's a correct observation. We Indians are prone to high morality. We may or may not put them into practice. Our high flown morals are not a part of our daily routine.'

She was mute for several moments and then spoke.

'Let me explain myself.'

'My clients engage me for household cleaning and pay for my sustenance. Moreover I am entitled to disability allowance.'

Avadhesha looked at her with a sense of relief.

'That's something wonderful in this country.'

'The government comes to the rescue of the aged and the disabled.'

She twitched her lips to form a smile.

'At times I do full service also.'

Avadhesha felt slightly taken aback and shook his foot-steps.

'Full service refers to brothels.'

This expression is implied suggestion of complete sexual activity in brothels.

'What do you imply by full service?'

'I deliberately used this word to tickle you. In my case it implies full cleaning of the house. I maintain a dog in my house. It takes care of me from unwanted visitors.'

Avadhesha had a feeling that the warning was meant for him.

'Don't be scared,' you can walk into my house whenever you want. I have a hobby also.'

Avadhesha was at the peak of curiosity.

'I attend writer's work-shop in Rockdale library.'

Avadhesha was once more amazed beyond bounds.

A cleaning girl attending writer's workshop!

He was finding it difficult to mentally adjust himself to the statement made by this lady. She sparked another bomb-shell upon him when she disclosed in grim tones that she was attempting to write a novel. Avadhesha was reminded of maid-servants in his own country. Most of them are hardly literate and have big families to support.

The sun-light had faded into nothingness. A heavy and cold-wind had come into existence from unknown corners.

Avadhesha glanced at her with a meaningful intent. She instantly understood and stepped towards him. It resulted into a very close hugging between the two. It continued for sometime. She separated herself from him and then looked into his eyes. After a few moments she scribbled her address and telephone number on a piece of paper and passed on to him. She slinked away to face the rough weather before catching some transport.

Avadhesha was almost breathless with excitement at warm embrace offered to him. He was feeling emotionally secure and ecstatic. He stepped outside the premises of the hospital with his mind brimming with something new and exciting.

11

It is almost a conclusion of great scientists like Freud that sub-conscious mind is a reservoir of our strong thoughts, emotions and feelings. It is like a group of glow-worms in pitch darkness. Scientists of the modern era associate it with past-life regressions, suppressed desires and pattern genes, responsible for unique, individual temperaments. For quite a few days Avadhesha was lost in the intimate and warm hug from Na-Dine. With the drifting time, she began to fade from his memory. But he could not ignore his immense inflanation for Irene. He must see her but her indifference towards him is likely to throw him into a boiling pit of mental torture. He must compensate his mental void with something substantial. Something looming vacancy in his life. He struck upon an idea. He must, in Sydney, visit some public libraries to pickup some intellectual activities.

Avadhesha decided to visit Kogar library not far from his residence. He entered the library and found the atmosphere quite congenial.

Avadhesha kept mum for a while and looking at different feminine faces sitting in the room. For sometime he kept looking around. Suddenly there was an announcement in the library that it was time for 'Book-Chat'. Any one interested in the 'Book-Chat' should enter room no 11. He immediately got up from his seat and headed towards room No. 11. He found quite a few ladies already seated inside the room. He felt a little fish out of water. He did not know what to say and whom to speak to.

After the collapse of some minutes a lady thirty years old stepped into the room. Her face was soft and smiling. She was well-built and her bosoms were quite attractive and plump.

'My name is Sophia. Hello, to each one of you. I have been entrusted with the job of handling 'Book-Chat. I welcome all of you.'

And she spread a wide smile on her face. She carried a bundle of books with her and softly put the books on the table.

'Have a look at them. It is a mix of British, Australian and many other famous authors of the world.' She proposed to discuss these authors with a gap of one month. Proposal is to discuss Emily Bronte's novel—'Withering Heights' after a gap of a month.'

She looked at the group to procure its approval. She cast a curious glance at Avadhesha. He too became aware of her attractive looks. Meanwhile many ladies nodded their approval. 'Book-chat' she resumed her talking—'is held in the library every Thursday of the weak between 12. PM to 1 PM. Apart from specific books, we can talk about general topics like Poetry, Novel, Historical Plays and many more aspects of creative writing and different literary genres of literature.'

She handed over to us typed programme of 'Book-Chat'. The paper carried an elaborate programme of the whole year. These was a bit of quiet in the company.

And then the entire set-up was accepted without an iota of any murmur.

'Thanks a lot Sophia. Quite a treat and repast for our reading and growth of knowledge.' One of the ladies spoke without any hesitation.

Avadhesha looked at her. Her name plate carried the name—'Barbara. She was a middle-aged lady. Her blooming youth was on a gradual decline. She searched for the response of the company and there seemed to be unison sweeping through their casual glances at Sophia. Her face was aglow with a dim smile. She once more picked up her drawl, 'I propose to arrange a tour of the library. It is likely to enlighten you a lot. You will be an acquaintance with the hidden corners of the library.'

The entire agenda was given nodding approval and was accepted by the company. The wall-clock struck 12 O'Clock and the room proceeded towards evacuation. Avadhesha was not in a hurry to leave the room. He thought of having an exchange of a few words with Sophia. She looked quite attractive and he was the only male in the entire lot. Sophia was busy giving final touches to collection of books and the coffee stand. He was left alone with her. She beamed a smile towards him.

'How do you like to Mr.?

'Avadhesha'.

'Avadhesha—it sounds quite difficult and difference. Never heard of such a name.'

'Quite correct. Its an Indian name. In Sydney two hundred and sixty languages are spoken. It is rather difficult to make out every culture, language and name.'

Sophia looked at him. While giving finishing touches to the coffee-stands.

'A . . . A . . . V . . . dasha . . . please don't mind. I can't pronounce Hindi word at all.'

'No problem,' it merely shows multicultural aspects of the city. The city is extremely sprawling.

'Multifarious regarding inhabitants and ways of life. But there is a lot of uniformity in the infrastructure of the city. Flow of life is diverse and its manifestations are divergent. Sophia kept on looking at Avadhesha and kept smiling and then raised an abrupt question

'How long have you been here?'

'I keep on coming and going. My maximum stay does not extend beyond six months.

'I appreciate you observation. It is quite keen and penetrating.'

'I, am a bit of writer also.

'Oh! That's fine and fantastic. How many books have you written?'

The two books—'Twilight and 'The Eclipsed' are quite relevant to your language and culture.'

'Oh . . . . That's fine and quite encouraging. Immensely encouraging.'

She had given last touches to her job in the room. Avadhesha was much lost in the conversation. He hardly noticed the departure of the inmates of the room.

Avadhesha stood facing Sophia and peeping into her eyes. She also took care not to blink her eyes. It was motivation for him to feel an impulse of excitement. She advanced towards him and took him in her arms. It was a great moment in Avadhesha's psyche. It was not less than a catalytic agent igniting the source of emotional glow. Avadhesha felt the warmth of Sophia's breaths and an intense emotion peeping through her eyes. She departed after the lapse of many moments.

Avadhesha peeped through the glass pane and located the horizon of the sky bemobbed by an endless trail of clouds. Being sensitive to changes in the aspects of nature, he grew restive and emotionally changed. What a petty and an exalted moment. It should have stretched into eternity. Did Avadhesha come across this kind of situation in his own country? Not to the stretch of his own memory. It has never been that spontaneous and effortless. Avadhesha at the moment was more than satisfied and filled with raw material of divinity. For 'Book-Chat' weakly routine in Kograh library. It would keep him mentally alive, fertile and in the company of books—a symbol and pioneer of civilization. Between animal and man stands the book.

In Sydney libraries are a part of common man's life. Men, women of all ages and school-children find some sort of mental shelter in libraries. In fact, these are cultural hubs of the city where many facilities are given. Newspapers, all sorts of magazines, books of all geners are made available to card-holders. From time to time writers are invited to libraries. Intellectual, literary discourses are delivered to select audience. Some libraries hold classes in English to teach grown up beginners in the language. It is to facilitate their stay in Australia. These libraries are a throb and vitality for an intellectual growth and it promotes readership.

Reading gives to us a healthy escape from tediums of routine life. It lifts us above our mundane routine and makes us perch mentally into new regions. It is an ever-lasting source of mental growth and frees us from clumsy and strong thoughts swimming into the sub-conscious and conscious layers of our minds.

'Libraries are a memory of mankind' a quote from one of Shaw's plays pictured in Avadhesha's mental sky-scape.

Every week a small group of readers sits in an allotted room. Every week an already announced topic is fixed for discussion. All the members of the 'Book-Chat' discuss the topic. It helps to illuminate hidden corners of the topic. Every month a book comes under discussion. Each one of us makes an effort to illuminate the details of the book leading us to the vicinity of books. In the book discussion a representative of the library is also present. He or she gives written directions to book-discussion. It is not supposed to stretch beyond an hour. Written questions regarding a particular book are readout to the audience. They are required to display their critical evidence of the book to interpret and understand the basic, underlying currents in the creation of the book.

A brief refreshment is put on the side-table for the consumption of the participants. One week a simmering conflict grew up between Avadhesha and a lady called Kathy. It was the outcome of difference of opinion on a particular topic.

Kathy couldn't stand being contradicted.

'Don't contradict me Avadhesha. I hold onto my point of view. It is my point of view. Authentic and most considered.'

She got up from her seat to assert her anger followed by her academic assertion.

'But this is not correct. Absolutely wrong. How can I accept your ill conceived literary concept? What you say is baseless.' Avadhesha grew a little vehement and assertive in his contradiction to the lady.

Kathy was incited and she pounced upon Avadhesha by saying, "The other day you kissed me on my left cheek.'

Avadhesha was extremely puzzled and baffled at the statement.

She charged him with another accusation, 'You need a girl friend and not a friend. I refuse to be your girl friend.'

'I never demanded the same. You are grossly mistaken.' Avadhesha tried to protect his middle-class Indian morals.

'Then why did you make the statement?' Kathy was aggressive in questioning.

'Which statement?'

Avadhesha was quite scarred.

'The one referring to inspiration for creativity you expressed yourself in the group.'

Kathy's lips were indicative of her anger. 'That was purely an academic conclusion. Lives of great authors and creators are full of such examples. For instance deep, intense relationships between Beatrice and Dante. It is said that Dante never talked to Beatrice but was creatively and passionately attached to her. His creativity touched new expansions, depths and the result was the creation of 'The Divine Comedy.'

'So you think yourself to be Dante. You live in a world of your own fancy.' Kathy's satirical tone was pungent and piercing.

'Oh, no, no, please do not work on such presumptions. I meant nothing beyond the psychology of creativity'.

'I don't believe you.'

'I can't forget the impression of your lips on my check.'

She vacated the room like a whirlwind.

Avadhesha got scarred and didn't know how to come out of the trap being weaved by Kathy. He felt extremely down-trodden and mentally depressed.

'Kathy is a pervert and of a very low psychological set-up,' he muttered to himself thereby intensifying his mental anguish.

Kathy, a plump lady, had met Avadhesha during a metro journey. An initiative of talking to her was taken by Avadhesha. It was just a month before. Indians by temperament are talkative and try to cultivate contacts even with strangers. In this country most of the people escape talking to strangers. They keep to themselves and keep themselves busy in different ways. This lady was quite prompting in talking to Avadhesha.

'Where do you live?' Avadhesha had asked her.

'In Kograh, in the vicinity of the library'.

'Oh! really? I visit the library once every week.

'To what purpose?' her curiosity was candidly written on her massive face. To attend 'Book-Chat'—an academic and a special feature of 'What's on in the library, why don't you come and join the clan? More the merrier.'

Avadhesha had opened the doors ajar for a new entrant. She seemed to have imbibed the idea to his heart's content.

'You forget to detail me the day and time.'

'Sorry, just did not click my mind. Your question implies that you have become a participant. It is every Thursday from twelve to one. The last Thursday of the month is reserved for 'Book-Chat' sponsored by the person incharge. You are most welcome.'

Kathy got down the train bidding good-bye to Avadhesha.

And now she was making tricky attempts at his exit from 'Book-chat'.

He questioned himself why of the situation. But was inable to locate any tangible answer to his heart. He kept on conjecturing all types of ugly ideas. She must have conveyed all sorts of misgivings about him thereby trying to malign his character. He felt just like a fish out of water and was feeling dumped down in feelings and thinking. He came out of the room to encounter the same group of ladies chattering and whispering to one another. On his arrival there was a kind of quiet. He stood up there mute and in a statue like state.

One of them shouted at him, 'Why do you come to attend 'Book-Chat?' To what purpose? You should listen more and talk less. You must give an opportunity to participant speakers.'

He was simply taken aback at the well planned and ill meant accusation hurdled at him.

He looked at the faces of those ladies and found them opaque and neutral to his feelings. He felt humiliated and down-trodden. Another lady eyed him with anger brimming in her eyes.

'Yes, I endorse Sophy in her striatum against you. You must mend your ways or you'll be constantly disowned by us.'

In an impulse of vexation he left the door ajar and quitted the premises. Kathy was there with two more ladies. He thought he might get a soft expression from them but they receded into an isolated corner to slight his exit.

His face was flushed and legs unsteady. Meanwhile strong whiffs of wind came into motion very unexpectedly. The sun had suddenly hid itself into the precincts of on rushing clouds. He sat down on one of the way-side benches and started pondering over the sinister consequence of the events.

He searched his pockets in desperation as he wanted to escape his present anguish. He lit a cigarette and stared into vacancy. He was in search of some kind of consolation but there was none available to him at the present moment.

Meanwhile a beautiful neatly dressed damsel came and sat near him on the same bench. He looked at her and picked up some spirit. He looked at her twice or thrice and she responded with a dim smile on her face. His feeling pitched buoyancy. But it was quite temporary. She was drowned in her cigarette and mobile. Avadhesha cast a critical glance at the deepening hue of the sky. There started a minor drizzle from the precincts of the overcast sky. In a huff he left the bench and proceeded in the direction of the station. Before boarding the train he was determined to pacify his restless soul and relentless sentiments kicking his psyche. He looked around and found himself standing at the threshold of a pharmacy. He entered the shop and a fair, young lady chirpped, 'What can I do for you? How can I help you?'

'You have glucose testing provision with you?'

'Let me ask,' and she was back in a moment.

'Please, sit down. Wait for sometime.'

He was glad to be seated there. After the lapse of a few minutes a Chinese girl swam into his ken with a broad smile on her face.

'Sir, you want your sugar checked?'

He nodded his assent very politely and beamed a broad smile at her that she cordially responded.

'How much the test cost?' he whispered rather slowly.

'No charges, sir, it is covered under national diabetes scheme.'

Avadhesha heaved a sigh of relief as he was unwilling to spend money following devalued Indian currency that he was supposed to spend in the form of Australian dollar.

'Which finger, sir?'

She leaned forward to reveal her bra-less breasts to his sight. His dwindling spirits picked up excitement and he forwarded his fore finger for blood testing. She caught hold of his finger and gave a soft prick. It amounted to a wonderful experience as he was having a full view of her breasts. Highly provocative sight and full of thrill. Chinese breasts? Breasts all over the world are same except some minor differences. But young breasts are a lot more provocative and sexy than declined breasts.

12

'Library is the memory of mankind'/a quote from Shaw's one of plays. It is an extremely valued statement in the advancement of human civilization. Books preserve knowledge in time and space writes C.E.M. Jood in his monumental book—'The Story of Civilization.'

The other day the sky was brightly lit with the sun-rays sprawling the earth in all its corners.

Well-illuminated libraries in Sydney are an academic asset for humanity. These libraries are wide spread net-work in the farflung precincts of the metropolis. These are not only beautiful habitats of books but a powerful help to cultural activities. These inspire all types of people keenly interested in all sorts of books and it is an incentive for readers to enter the realm of thought and beauty.

For instance in the State Library of Sydney, there is a marked room known as Shakespeare's Room, a magnificent tribute to the memory of a great bard and genius. Visitors are allowed to visit the room only on Tuesdays. The room carries sixteenth century ambience as the great poet and the dramatist belongs to this century. The room has ceiling with a sixteen-century design imparting it a shape. It came into existence with the elaborate contributions of Australian citizens in 1942.

Shakespeare wrote in all thirty eight plays of various geners like tragedy, comedy, historical plays and romances. His imaginative flights are global, universal and capture all shades of human nature. His characters include all types of characters universal in substance and human traits. Diversity of character is mind-boggling 'others abide our questions thou arts free' a poem dedicated to the creative genius of Shakespeare. The poem was composed by a Victorian poet, Matthew Arnold. The Shakespeare Room is a monumental in preserving all the dramas of the dramatists and it accommodates their translations almost in all languages of the world. Free tours are organized to this Room with a great pomp and show and outer decorations. It is commented that whenever a play is put on stage in any language in any part of the world, a part of Shakespeare is always there.

Avadhesha stood at the counter looking for a display of items on the screen. A bald-headed Australian was managing the counter. Avadhesha's sight caught an item of culture in room No. 114 of the library.

It seems to be an interesting item. Most probably it is a talk.

'Oh . . . . Yes . . . you may join if you so like. Some one is speaking on 'Abuses of Sex.'

The entry is free. Avadhesha was delighted at this piece of information and proceeded towards the room. It was on the 4th floor. He called the lift and reached his destination. He gave a slight push to the door of the room and quickly occupied a seat. The room accommodated an audience of nearly fifty inclusive of men and women. The speaker's accent was essentially Australian and he was speaking—'sex energy is of a vital importance and can be channelized into creative channels. It can be profusely abused by misdirection. It can be relegated if we over-look its proper direction.'

There was a sudden break in the flow of the speaker. The organizer of the congregation intervened and invited the audience to coffee.

Avadhesha found himself in the company of unknown faces including the speaker. The assembly of the audience got busy in sipping coffee and chewing eatables. The coffee-break was quite rewarding and tasty as it offered some sumptuous snacks also. Avadhesha was immensely glad to be an integral part of the proceedings of the party.

Eatings were interrupted by small chats and light giggles. Everyman was managing himself. Avadhesha was reminded of the status of the chief guest of any assembly in India. He is accorded a lot of respect and fill attention. Refreshments are offered to him in a very special and courteous manner. He is looked after as a man of exceptional space at least for the duration of the function. And then he is welcomed and given a special welcome on the stage. Invariably he is garlanded at the entrance of the function. He is presented memento on the stage. Avadhesha looked at the chief guest of the present function. He sat down in one of the counters of the room munching the stuff of his choice in a plate picked up by himself. Avadhesha felt dazed at the cultural contrast of two countries from where do cultural roots of a country or a community or a nation sprout? He fell into a deep pondering.

Almost amazing that humans of all over the world have same basic instincts. But their transformation into sound social habits takes diverse directions.

The audience resumed their seats in order to listen to the speaker. His voice was eloquent and vivid. The audience gave to him full attention and some of them were taking notes. The speaker's voice drawled out—'It is essential to give proper channels to our sex energy. Its implications should be properly appreciated, imparted in right perspects. Wrong channelization of sexual energy may grow into something morbid and deformed. It should not be experimental. This is the only way to have a mature and creative attitude towards sexual energy. This energy can be sublimated into higher dimensions and impartial creative channels leading to the progress of civilization and humanity.' He gave a pause to a discreet drawl which was followed by a brief clapping.

The organizer of the function stood up and spoke rather politely and dimly, 'you are welcome to ask any question. Mr. Howard will be glad to answer your queries. Time allowed to the question session is fifteen minutes. After the question, you are invited to lunch.'

Avadhesha felt quite happy at the announcement. Free coffee and then free lunch—a purposeful spending of time in nice direction.

A woman stood up—'How can we pass on vital information regarding sexual energy to our teenagers? We feel shy to discuss the matter with them?'

'The best alternative is to suggest some good books to them. That will pep up their healthy curiosity. And if they persist with questions no harm holding discussion on them.'

The woman reoccupied her seat in silence.

A man rather aged in looks and voice looked up from his seat—'What about the aged? At times we feel the acute urgency for indulgence in sexual intercourse. The body cries for it. But we are loners with our wives divorced.'

Mr. Howard looked at the personage asking this question had said—'Your question is human and genuine. Suppression of any instinct leads to morbidity and a mental chaos. For you the best is to find out a partner. The last resort is brothel. At least you can gain relief.'

The question hour came to an abrupt close. Avadhesha was fully and mentally prepared to enjoy a sumptuous lunch. He was reminded of his visits to Sahitya Academy in New Delhi. The writers and the audience are freely fed. Festival of Letters' comprising of many sessions of discussions on various aspects of literature and then tea or lunch according to the hours.

At least they maintain the good tradition of feeding the audience. He was certain of these certainties. He stood in the queue to lunch in an adjoining room. He stepped up to enter the room.

A polite voice checked him, 'Sir, your name and registration?'

'Registration? To what purpose? I can't understand your implication.'

'I'm sorry. The lunch is pre-paid and must have been registered.'

'Oh, I see.'

'Sorry, sir, please don't mind. It's our common custom.'

Avadhesha was wonder-struck. He stepped out of the queue and with a confused mind entered the toilet.

After finishing his physical obligation he returned to the organizer.

'But, sir, in our country in such literary meets eatings are free.'

'Sorry sir, we don't have that facility here. Here free events are very rare.'

'Oh, really!' Avadhesha did not deem it proper to follow the argument. He took a step towards the exit where his glance caught the main speaker (the chief guest) ready to depart from the room. Avadhesha was perplexed at the sight of the chief guest.

'My God!—the chief quest lingering in a corner?'

Avadhesha could not escape his curiosity.

'Sir, what about your chief guest?

'I'm afraid he also does n't have his registration.'

An imaginative incarnation of the chief guest of his country rose before his eyes.

13

It was 10.30 in the morning. The 'service' in the Uniting Church, Rockdale was receiving last touches in terms of a cup of tea. A small gathering consisting of all nationalities talking in diverse languages on diverse topics. A small gathering of all ages ranging from ten to ninety nine years in age—cold drinks, coffee, biscuits were being consumed by one and all.

'Hello Avadhesha! How do you do?' An elderly lady addressed him.

He confronted the lady with a genuine smile across his face.

'I'm fine. How about you Rosy? I'm glad to see you. Did you go through my novel?

'Yes . . . . I did read your novel. You write well. Your expressions in English are creative and suggestive. I congratulate you.' She spoke in her dim voice, with a faint smile on her wizened face. Avadhesha cast a critical glance at her figure.

A thin lean body! Her face was crowded and bemobbed by zig-zag wrinkles. Her teeth did not show any decline or decay. But her eyes had lost her luster and there gleamed a kind of dimness in them.

Avadhesha was propelled by Indian culture and felt like touching her feet in reverence but checked himself dictated by Sydney culture and manner of accosting.

He addressed her reverentially—'Hello Rosy, I hope you are keeping well. Thanks for your encouraging observations regarding my book. I hope you are keeping fit.'

'Of course, of course. I'm keeping well. You know how old am I?'

An iota of pride was visible on her face. She looked at him with a dimbly conceived smile like a candle in pitch darkness. Avadhesha nodded his head in mild negation regarding the estimate of her age. He got a bit confused and helpless and was lost in wondering speculation about her age. She could surmise the contempt of Avadhesha's speculation. She spoke rather in candid tones, 'I'm ninety nine years old.'

And she stood still like a statue with Monaliza's smile on her face.

Avadhesha once more looked at her and glared at the main contours of her face that carried the burden of ninety nine years of aging process. They appeared to Avadhesha marked evidence of her advanced years. Avadhesha thought of the aged in his own country. They seldom cross the threshold of eighty and wither away into nothingness.

'Are you absolutely alone in the world?'

'No . . . no . . . I have one brother and one sister. They are also unmarried and aged like me. Off and on we exchange visits but not very frequently. It is because we live apart from one another in terms of distance but not emotionally. We derive immense pleasure whenever we communicate or meet one another but such occurrence are rare. Telephonically we avoid any journey to meet one another?' Rosy spoke and eyed at Avadhesha very dimly.

'Did you enjoy the novel 'Twilight' that you bought from me?'

She tried to talk her forgetfulness.

'In fact, I am fond of reading many books. That's why 'Twilight' is missing my mind. Yes, I recall now. It is regarding criminalization of Indian politics.'

'Exactly, Exactly'.

Avadhesha repeated the words to manifest his excitement at the mention of his book. He felt a bit flattered and secure when his book was mentioned. Avadhesha requested the old lady to sit down on chair and discuss her life in general.

'You are interested in my mode of living? I cook and clean. I eat and digest. That's also time consuming.'

'Why not? Why not?'

'How about your neighbours?'

'It's a colony of ten houses accommodating one inmate in each house.'

'Do they converse with you? Do they visit you?'

'Not very often'. The old lady was not feeling relaxed.

'It's not that formal as you are likely to presume. If by chance anyone comes across you, you can talk to him. Rarely they walk into houses and share their feelings.'

The church Hall was thinning down with people existing it.

But Avadhesha and Rosy kept sitting on their seats.

'What about your sex life Rosy?

Avadhesha himself felt embarrassed at his own question. How could he dare? In his own country, at least he would have received shoe beating and invectives from the lady. Rosy brought a beaming smile on her face and spoke, 'It's nice of you ask me this intimate question. You have pushed me back to my old memories.?'

There appeared a sort of brightness on her face.

'Sweet remembrance of three partners. I tasted sex life with each one of them to the fullest extent.'

There was no moral hassal on her face. She seemed to be dwelling in the experience. She looked at Avadhesha to register his reaction. He was feeling wide awakened at the mention of the sequence. But it was not the end of the story. Rosy put down the cup of coffee on the nearby table and resumed the narrative.

'You see, initial years of my uni-education expenses were met by my presence in brothels in Sydney. Quite paying and satisfying also. Killing two birds with one stone.'

'Your parents?'

'Our social set-up is different. For our uni-expenses all means are legal and moral. No stigma to anything. No gender discrimination.'

'Rosy, in your youth you must be pretty.'

'I don't know. Yes, now I recollect also. I was quite pretty and there are changes at a steady pace and sometimes it happens all of a sudden. But in a way my life was a gradual decline. I suffered from no disease except curable minor ailments.'

Rosy's voice was mild yet firm. It was the voice of recollections. But it was not tinged with any regret.

Avadhesha imagined the precarious situation of her life. If she is taken ill at night, no one is there to help her.

She munched her teeth and then spoke in soft tones, 'I'm used to my loneliness. I cook my food once in a day and try to keep myself busy by making nuttings for fingers.'

Avadhesha glanced at her face beaming a tinted smile—'Wheelchair food sent by Rockdale council.'

'Free?'

'Nothing is free in Sydney except the sun-set and sun-rise. Rates of Rockdale Wheelchair food are not very expensive. The rates are quite affordable. I pay for my food. It avoids a lot of bothersome activities connected with cooking. Moreover my eye-sight is quite weak. I have all sorts of fears. I may damage any part of my body.'

Avadhesha kept on staring at her face. A kind of stoicism was writ in her wrinkles. She twitched her lips to express something but nothing tangible came out of her lips.

'Aren't you afraid of loneliness? How do you manage to sleep all alone in the house without the presence of any human being? Suppose something happens to you.'

She couldn't furnish a prompt reply to his apprehensive assertion. She took sometime to frame an answer to his question. Avadhesha cast a glance at the hall being deserted by ladies and gents. Only one door was half-open. Rest of the enclosure was about to shut. She looked around and made a bid towards the door. Avadhesha followed her fervently as he was keen to have her answer.

'At night I'm not all alone. Christ is with me to protect me. I have lived with Holy Spirit throughout my life and in eternity I propose to live with it. I'm bound to have his pity and protection.'

They had already left the big building behind.

Who says that the West does not live by religious faith? The East has an erroneous view. Faith is a psychological necessity. Man can't live an external life. Why? It is because he is bound to go into abstractions because of the presence of neuronr's in his brain.'

Avadhesha was talking to himself only.

'Rosy, do you mind if we sit on the road-side bench and talk?'

'Oh, no, I wouldn't mind.'

'It's quite interesting to converse with you.'

They perched on the road-side bench and resumed there talking despite the constant flow on the road. The weather was changing its hues after the collapse of some moments. Life is a kind of influx, a constant change creeps in our life. Basic elements of life are also in a state of motion and change. Rosy gave a massive assent to what Avadhesha had uttered aloud. Her dim eyes were in kind of glow. She produced something before Avadhesha.

'What is this? A photograph?. It is a group photograph. Simply wonderful. Can you locate me in the group-photograph? No? Let me put my finger on my photograph.'

'You are surrounded by children?'

'Yes, war victims in second world war. I was put as an incharge of a hut full of children.'

'A big social service?'

'You can talk like that. I took care of the children in the house, where they lived during the second world war.'

'You seem rather quite healthy in the group photograph. It hardly resembles you. Its absolutely different.'

Avadhesha uttered a line from T.S. Eliot's poem—'Where is the life, we have lost in living?'

Rosy looked at him and spoke softly.

'Avadhesha, Time doesn't spare any one born on the planet—the earth. It passes by slowly put certainly. It changes us absolutely. But there is something eternal in us.'

'Yes, that's correct. I have read some Indian saints. We learn a lot from them. They talk about the immortality of human soul.'

'You seem to be quite familiar with our approach to human life.'

'Yes, quite vividly.'

'You read fiction as well as non-fiction.'

'I can imagine that. I appreciate your love for reading books.'

'You know . . . .'

She did not complete her sentence but kept on blinking her eye-lids.

'You did n't complete your sentence.'

'I meant to say that I am the author of a book.'

'Splendid' Avadhesha spoke in amazement. Title of the book?'

'Crossing the Continent.'

'Simply beautiful.'

'It is non-fiction. It tells about the spans of second world war and predicament of children during the war.

'I wrote it long back. Later on I added more matter to the book. A few months back, it was launched by the Governor of the state. It was a glamorous moment for me. I was given a massive appreciation for the book written by me.'

Avadhesha was highly impressed by the glow on her face. It was primarily because of the V.I.P. treatment as an authoress. It was a matter of great pride for her to get personal attention from the Governor in Sydney. Avadhesha thanked Rosy porously for staying back with him in such an awesome weather.

14

It was not yet 10 O'Clock and Avadhesha was walking towards Hartsville library. He had a mind to attend the meeting of a club known as Friends of Hartsville library. Avadhesha was quite excited at the prospect of meeting international community. It is always a pleasure to meet people from diverse nationalities because it enlarges our vision and human understanding about the world. We have an acute realization that humanity is made of the same stuff and is propelled by the same instincts and propensities. The doors of the library were not yet open. A cool breeze was in slow motion imparting a tinge of cold to the atmosphere. Many visitors stood at the threshold of the library waiting for the opening hours of the library. Avadhesha patiently sat down on a cemented seat at the entrance of the library. A chirrpy silence existed in the atmosphere. Suddenly he traced a woman sitting in his vicinity. He cast an intimate glance at her to gain a few patches of conversation with her. He observed that she was not in her usual mood. On the other hand she kept up her calm of mind undisturbed.

Avadhesha maintained his occasional gaze at her for several seconds and then slowly uttered Hello.'

Her lips made a slow movement and responded to 'hello.'

'Waiting for the library to open?'

'Yes, yes. I'm a bit early. I have to return and withdraw some books.'

She spoke slowly. Her middle-aged face was slightly taut and tension-ridden.

'You belong to which country?' A sudden question born out of vacancy was sprung at Avadhesha. He was glad at the question as it paved way for further conversation.

'India. I'm visiting my son and daughter. They live here I visit them almost every year.'

'That's wonderful,' she displayed a bit of excitement and a sort of flow surfaced her chubby cheeks. She belonged to the middle rank of her age and her hair were bobbed.

'In fact, shortly I am visiting India.'

'But when?' Avadhesha displayed his curiosity.

'After a fortnight. My flight is reserved. I'm bound for New Delhi.

'Where do you stay in New Delhi? In a hotel?'

'Oh, no, no, An expression of defection appeared on her face.

'Then?'

'With an Indian family. They are pally with me. Extremely. The are a Singh family. They take care of my needs'.

'Vow!' Avadhesha tried a to be modern in outlook.

'The family takes care of me, not only physically but emotionally also.'

'How?'

'I'm treated one among them. Every year I go to meet them. It is primarily to beat the loneliness of Sydney. It is to feel the warmth of human emotion. It's missing here, yes, missing here.'

Avadhesha felt like contradicting her but kept quiet because of the annoyed curves on her forehead. He thought it better to give a silent assent to what she narrated.

'Bastard . . . . !' The expression was vivid, abrupt and had sprung from no contextual regime.

'Yes, he was a bastard to me. To begin with, he would batter me every night, undress me completely and then batter me. Then he would stride away to a brothel. For a few days I allowed him his perversity and then it went beyond me.'

Avadhesha felt extremely confused at what the lady spoke to him. Her face glistened with drops of perspiration. She seemed to be feeling extremely distraught.

'It's alright to drink and to visit a brothel but why to beat me? Heartless beast . . .'

'To whom are you referring to?

'Obviously to my husband. We got married. I gave my body, I earned money for him. With my earnings he drank and prostituted.'

'Oh . . . . God . . . . I thought everything is nice in Sydney.'

'It's novice of you to think like this.'

She wiped her forehead off the sweat.

'I'm sorry.'

'You need not . . . . No.'

Human society is not perfect. Somewhere it is cankerous life. Life can not be completely ethical. It goes towards deformity also.

Avadhesha felt awed at the erudition and wisdom of the lady. She was not in a hurry.

Meanwhile the doors of the library were flung afar. But Avadhesha and the lady kept sitting on the cemented perch of the enterace.

'And one night, I felt enraged beyond my rationality. I pounced upon my husband. I beat him blue and black. He kept crying and wailing. But not a drop of mercy oozed from my total being. I threw him out my house like a bundle of garbage.'

'Brave of you.'

'Brave of me. I felt no remorse. I did not allow him to reenter my house. He filed the divorce papers. We consented to live away from each other.'

'I simply marvel at your spirit of relationship. One day you have to fight. Even a weak and tiny creature can grow revengeful. How long can we tolerate cruelty and inhumanity?'

She paused and then spoke, 'I'm taking twenty books to India.'

'For selling?'

'She gave a bright smile.

'No, for reading.'

Avadhesha was beaten with curiosity.

'Reading is the best medium of relaxation. It refreshers our nerves. It imparts a vital, new energy to our system. Avadhesha grew thoughtful. In his country the neglect of book is rather amazing. Instead of reading books they indulge in malicious gossip. Their minds travel into the hidden corners of deformity but not into realms of beauty and expression. The lady seemed to be quietened but a powerful storm was raging in her mind.

Her foot steps indicated a jittery movement. She seemed to be on the verge of departure.

'Before you go, please tell me your name if you don't mind.'

'Margeret,' I'm working in a garment store. I have already separated myself from my husband. He has given me no child because his primary love was brothels. He prostituted of all ages satisfying his lust.'

'I have all sympathies with you Margeret, human life is not a straight line. There are curves. Sometimes curves are very intricate and tedious. They bring massive defeat for us and we are dismissed like a pack of garbage. How does that Sikh family accommodate you? I don't think people in my country are that innocent and simple.'

'Quite true, not much differences among human beings. I take for them precious gifts from Sydney. Then feel much pleased with them. Well, human life is nothing but trading. It's rare that people don't expect anything in compensation.'

Margeret was in a big hurry, she was about to depart. She handed over a card to Avadhesha and bade him an affectionate good-bye with a brief kiss on his check.

He felt quite enlivened. No Indian woman would kiss him with this brief span of introduction and conversation, she left Avadhesha in a mood of deep contemplation. Perfection is almost impossible to achieve in a community or a country. There are abbreisations leading human beings to pit-fells.

'Brothel' an integral and important aspect of Sydney. It is a manifestation of Kamasutra of India. A powerful, natural instinct pervading in all the species of the world. It inevitably brings the two sexes in unison despite moral and social protestations. The basic instinct leading to the perpetuation of any species. Avadhesha tried to philosophize the basic instinct. In Daily Telegraph and many other news papers of Sydney brothels are displayed with tempting details. Quite tempting and unresistable if your pockets can afford it. It is a legal way to channelize your sexual energies. It is morbid to indulge in sexual perversions but these are becoming rampant in the west. It is rather unfortunate and a road to perversity.

Avadhesha entered the portals of the library. Everything was spick and span and rows of books were trim and in symmetry. An extremely congenial atmosphere to study and to be contemplative. Time to be oblivious of the dull routine of life and enhance our consciousness on a different plain of ascendance. Yes, he must attend the meeting of friends of Hurstville library. It is a good assembly of members and guests.

A well-managed space with chairs in rows. A screen is there to capture the pictures of the projector used by almost all authors who come and lecture in the hall.

Invariably they bring their books for display and selling. At least one is bought by the president of the club. Sometimes members and guests also buy books. Avadhesha observed the proceedings of the club. He found himself in a distinctly different atmosphere permeated with intellectual oozings.

A beautiful blonde was there to represent Hurstville library. She was beautifully clad and played an active role in the proceedings of the meet.

The meeting was called to an order. The president and the secretary of the club were seated in their proper places. The minutes of the previous meeting were read out and duly approved by the house. Details of the income and expenditure of the previous meeting were tabled in the meeting. It was approved with a thumping majority. The president, a thin and lean man got up.

'Thank you very much for approving the minutes of the last meeting.'

He handed over the report of the previous meeting to the representative of the library. She spoke rather politely, 'Thank you very much. A part of the report will appear in the monthly pamphlet of the library.'

The secretary, an old lady, announced, 'Time for coffee break.' Every body got up and proceeded towards the table of refreshments. Prior to this they had contributed three dollars to the refreshment fund.

Eating and talking were concentrating. It was a congenial atmosphere. It was a very small assembly of international community including members and guests.

Two Chinese girls came near Avadhesha and addressed him 'To-day your lecture?'

'Oh, no, no lecture but reading from my latest novel, 'The Migrant'.

'Yes, yes, We caught the reference of the meet from 'Leader'.

'Leader is the source of your information. I'm glad that you have come to attend the meet.'

'Thank you very much.'

After refreshment Avadhesha came on the dias read out from his 'The Migrant.' To the audience it gave a philosophical flavour interwoven with strong story element. The audience was kept spell-bound and absorbed in the narrative. It continued for forty five minutes. After the narration of the novel was over a brief ceremony of thanks giving followed accompanied by thunderous clapping. Avadhesha felt exalted and elevated in his mental equipment to him it was a god-sent opportunity to give a boost to his creative fervour.

It was a unique mental experience to him, a significant experience in a foreign strand.

A fat, chubby nosed gentleman stepped on the dias. He handed over a card to Avadhesha.

'Thank you very much Avadhesha. A fine experience to listen to you! Really an interesting beginning of the novel. We are delighted at your presence. Before I resume my seat, I want to raise a question'.

Avadhesha expressed his curiosity through his total expression of eyes and face.

'How can every one be of equal mental growth and state in the world?'

Avadhesha brought a faint smile on his face, 'sir, I never meant your implication. I referred to basic human instincts. Culture comes into existence when we transform and sublimate our instincts into social habits to suit a particular social and climatic social set-up and environment.'

Another wave of clapping and it came to a civilized ending.

15

$$\sim$$

Avadhesha sat in a small park escorted and surrounded by a constant flow of humanity on Sydney roads. It was the dawn of evening lit by neon tubes in the close vicinity of shadowing trees. He looked here and there to locate spots of beauty to mentally inhale the entire spectrum. He lit a cigarette and tried to be mentally isolated and introspective. Flow of life is individual as well as collective. Our consciousness is divided in many vistas having a crescendo of feelings and emotions. There are mental valleys as well as hill tops. Hill topes sometimes look blackened and sometimes snowy. Avadhesha's mind was in a subdueed motion pertaining to the influx of unconscious.

'O . . . . he espied a queue of five people on the threshold of the pub visible within his visible ken. 'And why do they stand in a queue?' The door of the pub was ajar. Avadhesha's eyes traveled the entire view and found a beautiful girl—the nucleus of the entire sight.

The blonde was extremely capturing and offered kisses on her lips. For Avadhesha it was thrill to look at the situation. Yes, they were offering her price of the event. She needed money to feed herself and keep herself slim and trim and maintain her attractiveness. In the park there was an other bench occupied by two middle-aged human beings. Avadhesha looked at them furtively. 'My God! They seemed to be of equal ages.'

Were they in conversation with each other? Of course not. They seemed to be of distinct relationships.

Looks reveal our identities to some extent.

Avadhesha concentrated on the emerging contours of their faces. One of them belonged to Australia and the other one seemed to be an Indian. Avadhesha's stare at the Indian intensified as he was trying not to look at the female figure at the entrance of the pub.

'Quite interesting and intriguing, Avadhesha spoke to himself and secretly smiled at the situation. The Australian was staring at the girl without blinking his eyes. His face did not register an iota of moral calamity.

Avadhesha could see his eyes floating in the direction. Suddenly he stood up, searched the pockets of his upper garment and proceeded in the direction of the pub.

He walked towards the pub casting absolutely no secret or sly expression on his face staring towards the pub and approaching the girl. He forwarded the money to the girl, held her cheeks in his hands and implanted a deepand lasting kiss on her lips. He was thrilled to have the touch of the young girl. A revival of youth! It must be a wonderful experience. Avadhesha thought and gave a delicate movement to his lips. Yes, he too should under go this experience. What is wrong about it? Nothing wrong. Just a bargain of five dollar note. He looked intently at the other middle-aged man. Looks like from India? thought Avadhesha. He made up his mind to talk to the man but put a restrain on his impulse. In case he introduced himself he is likely to the park.

He did not want to deprive him of the pleasure he might try to attain by kissing the girl. The Indian middle-aged man seemed to be in a mental strife. It was not what Hamlet felt 'To be or not to be' . . . . 'To kiss or not to kiss.'

Avadhesha conjectured that he must be thinking of his village environment in India.

Daughters and daughters-in-law going towards the village with their heads properly covered with their aprons. They feel shy and shrink away at the appearance of an elderly man.

Avadhesha could perceive the internal mental conflict be mobbing his thinking. The middle-aged man derived consolation from many factors. His wife was situated at a distance of ten thousand kilometers from Sydney. His own identity was absolutely unknown. To the best of his knowledge no Indian was nearby. What a golden opportunity! The old man's psyche suddenly was in a grip and he would certainly be watched by God. He was likely to punish him after his departure from this planet.

The elderly personage thought that he must make some divine provision to escape this calamity heaped by on him. To touch another girl than his own wife, was a gross sin.

He must escape the consequences of the sin and experience a thrilling of kissing another girl than his own wife. She was an Australian girl. She must be tasting differently. It must be a heavenly experience. He mused and mused and then hit upon a plan to escape the dire consequences he was likely to pile upon him as a sinner.

Avadhesha was keenly watching the movements of the Indian. He could surmise his moral and social set-up because he himself hailed from the same social and moral set-up.

Moral hassles leading to conflicts in Indian psyche are bound to be there. Time and again it is dinned into that sex is gross sin. He is not given a healthy and acceptable view of the situation.

The middle-aged Indian moved to an adjoining bench at a little distance from other benches. He sat down in the manner of Indian saint and started reciting some incantations. There was a slow but steady movement of his lips. His recitation of mantras was hardly audible.

He kept on sitting in the same posture for five minutes and then left the bench. He gave a slow search to his pockets and made himself certain of the money he possessed. Then he cast furtive glances in the manner of a fugitive. A moral bewilderment and consciousness of guilt were largely writ on his face. Avadhesha was psychologically in the grip of the Indian's psyche.

His facial and other movements betrayed that he was passing through valleys of moral darkness.

Avadhesha located him going in the direction of the pub with unsteady strides. Hesitation was writ on his face. Before approaching the girl he made a minor halt as if to enter the danger zone. He saw him going in the direction of the pub with unsteady strides. Hesitancy was visible on his legs. Before approaching the girl he made a minor halt as if to survey the danger zone before taking the last leap. Yes—he was there. Avadhesha laughed in kiss sleeves. May be that he was perspiring. Avadhesha could see him leaning on the face of the girl. His fingers did not grip her checks passionately and firmly. He advanced his lips towards the lips of the girl and then registered a halt. But the suspension was purely temporary. Then he caught hold of the girl's face and apologetically kissed her.

He nervously fumbled his pockets and extracted a five dollar note and game it to the girl. She uttered 'thank you very much.' I bade him good bye with a mischievous smile. The Indian came back to his previous perch like some one victorious in a battle field.

The Australian sitting nearby him spoke to him. It's not hot! Perspiring how come did n't you enjoy the performance? He nodded his head in assent with a false laughter on his face.

THE END